TARZAN and the Revolution

Eric Benton, an idealistic young Midwestern Peace Corps volunteer, could hardly have known that his mission to help an African village would embroil him and his colleagues in the political struggles of an emerging African nation.

The people of central Africa likewise had no idea how quickly their expectations for freedom could be taken away when a ruthless dictator seizes power.

And Tarzan of the Apes had no idea that before long, he would be compelled, once again, to undertake a long and perilous journey with the Waziri to save their families.

Set against a backdrop of political unrest in modern Africa, Thomas Zachek's latest page-turner takes the reader from the dank treasure troves of the lost city of Opar to turmoil in the city streets as Tarzan battles one of his most ruthless foes!

PUBLISHED BY

Edgar Rice Burroughs, Inc., Tarzana, California

TARZAN AND THE REVOLUTION™

THE WILD ADVENTURES OF EDGAR RICE BURROUGHS® SERIES

TARZAN AND THE REVOLUTION™

THOMAS ZACHEK

COVER & INTERIOR ILLUSTRATIONS

BY

MIKE GRELL

EDGAR RICE BURROUGHS, Inc.
Publishers
TARZANA   **CALIFORNIA**

Tarzan and the Revloution
First Edition

Trademarks including Tarzan®, Edgar Rice Burroughs® and
Tarzan and the Revolution ™ owned by
Edgar Rice Burroughs, Inc.
Cover art and interior illustrations by Mike Grell
© 2018 Edgar Rice Burroughs, Inc.

Special thanks to Bob Garcia, Gary A. Buckingham, Joan Bledig,
John Martin, Mike Conran, Scott Tracy Griffin, and Tyler
Wilbanks for their valuable assistance in producing this novel.

Number 8 in the Series

Library of Congress CIP (Cataloging-in-Publication) Data
ISBN-13:
978-1-945462-18-4

- 9 8 7 6 5 4 3 2 1 -

TO THE READER

You hold in your hands a new Tarzan novel.

Since Edgar Rice Burroughs created the character more than a hundred years ago, Tarzan of the Apes has become one of the most enduring characters in all of popular fiction. In addition to the original twenty-six novels, the character has been popularized for decades in movies, television programs, comics, Disney animated features, and even a Broadway musical.

This is my second Tarzan book, after *Tarzan Trilogy*, published in 2016. I am one of a privileged group of writers licensed by Edgar Rice Burroughs, Inc., to write new stories about our hero to add to the Greystoke legacy. Others include Will Murray, Gary Buckingham, Michael Sanford, Ann Johnson, and Ralph Laughlin.

As an author trying to create new stories for such a well-established character, I am inclined to try new directions, approaches, and storytelling styles. This story is set in the latter half of the Twentieth Century, and the Tarzan of this story is an older man who sees the Africa of his younger days changing in many ways. He is called out of semi-retirement to aid his adopted tribe, the Waziri, one more time.

It features a visit to the ancient, mysterious lost city of Opar. It has flashbacks to Tarzan's earlier years. It also involves a group of young Peace Corps volunteers who become embroiled in the unfolding events.

You may already be familiar with the Lord of the Jungle, perhaps one of the thousands of devoted fans who have kept the Burroughs flame burning over the decades. I believe you will find my Tarzan solidly in the Burroughs tradition, and I hope you will be rewarded with an exciting and satisfying tale.

Along the way, perhaps you will also find something new to ponder. It is all any author can hope for.

But perhaps you are new to the Tarzan universe. Even if you are unfamiliar with the backstory of our hero and his many exploits, I believe you will find this tale accessible and compelling. And I hope it will spark your interest in further exploring the amazing and wondrous worlds of Edgar Rice Burroughs.

I welcome any comments and feedback you have. You can email me at zachekbooks@gmail.com.

My thanks to Jim Sullos and the staff at ERB, Inc., for giving me this opportunity.

My gratitude to my faithful readers Lin Courchane, Chris Schoggen, and Dan Roskom for their willingness to read all my drafts and their enthusiastic encouragement. My gratitude also to Peter Lee, who served in the Peace Corps in Thailand, for his valuable background and information about Peace Corps life.

And my thanks and appreciation to my wife Amy for all her support.

Thomas Zachek
Menomonee Falls, WI
January, 2018

TABLE OF CONTENTS

Prologue

From the journal of Eric Benton, September 30, 1974:

> *Tomorrow we leave for Africa. I still can't believe it. To be accepted, to be actually going. No turning back now.*
>
> *All the preliminaries are finished. The long application process, the background check, the physical. More than I expected. Plus three months of training on the UW-Madison campus—four hours a day of language training, four hours a day of skills training. Whew. But after all that, I'm still excited, still pumped to go.*
>
> *I wonder what I'll be doing in a month, six months, a year from now?*
>
> *Scott says I should keep a journal and write down what I see and do and think. He says it might be interesting and valuable to look back on. He says the Peace Corps changes you. So I'm going to try. We'll see how it goes, I guess.*

Eric Benton paused to look up from his desk and found himself staring out his second-story bedroom window at the split-level homes, the manicured lawns, and the white sidewalks of his Oshkosh, Wisconsin, subdivision. He was trying to think of what to write next in his journal when the final chord of *Sgt. Pepper's* sounded and the turntable arm lifted off. He walked over to the stereo, plucked out his cassette, and slid it into its case. He was just placing the record back onto the shelf next to the Dylan, the Airplane, and the Fleetwood Mac LP's when he heard a rap on the doorway behind him and the soft voice of his mother saying, "Hey, there, whatcha doing?"

He turned and said to her, "Just finishing up dubbing

my records to tapes. I think I've got enough." Eric was five-foot-nine, slim of build, with unruly brown hair. His high cheekbones and dark brown eyes sometimes gave him an air of seriousness beyond his twenty-two years.

"How are you going to play them with no electricity?" she said.

"Batteries, Mom, batteries."

His mother stepped into the bedroom bedecked with rock music posters and high school band awards. The woman in her forties, with slightly disheveled brown hair, print housedress, and the beginnings of worn features, looked around the room. She noted the bookshelves straightened and the desktop cleaned off, and said, "So, are you all packed?"

"I think so," Eric said. He pointed to the suitcase and duffel bag on the end of the bed.

She respectfully poked through the contents of the open duffel for a moment. His suitcase had been carefully packed and bound with netting to protect against rough transit, as instructed.

"Is that going to be enough?"

"It'll have to be, Mom. Forty pounds. That's it," her son said, smiling.

"Well, take a break and come on down. Your father's home and dinner's ready."

She hesitated a moment, drawing a breath, and then continued, "Are you sure you're doing the right thing?"

Eric stopped to look up at her. "Mom. We talked about this. It's decided. I can't change it now. And, yes, it's the right thing."

"But it's so far. And it could be dangerous. Isn't there another way?"

"Another way to do what? That war is still going on, and you know the draft could be reinstated at any time. Now that I've graduated from college, I lose my deferment, but I'm still 1-A, and nobody in town wants to hire 1-A's. I can't afford grad school right now. Dad wants me to serve my country, but I'm not going to fight in that damn war I don't believe in. So, what are my options? Would you rather I ran off to Canada?

At least in the Peace Corps, I can feel that I'm doing some good. I want to see the real world. I want to be able to help people, make a difference. That's what President Kennedy said we need in the world, remember? And it's only for two years. I'll be back."

He felt he had recited that speech almost from memory. He had made those points a dozen times in the past two months, to family and friends. He knew that his mother accepted his decision rationally, but in her heart, she was still troubled. She recognized his maturity but still remembered the eight-year-old who had been reluctant to ride his bike more than six blocks away. She knew very little about Africa, and what she had heard was worrisome: disease, dictators, revolutions, the dangers of the wilderness, and so much crushing poverty. The land was so big, so mysterious. She did not know what to expect, and she feared the unknown.

Eric knew that there was only so much he could say to calm her fears, but he also knew that no matter what, she would let him go.

He smiled the winning grin that his mother had always loved. Taking her thin shoulders in his arms, he looked into her eyes and added, "I'm just going to try to help people. Isn't that a good thing? What could happen?"

Chapter 1

INTERVIEW

J ohn Clayton sat on his spacious veranda and gazed out over the magnificent African landscape that stretched before him to the north and west. The early afternoon sun glistened off the waters of the river in the distance that meandered through acres of open plains and grassy vistas dotted with clusters of boulders and patches of scrub trees.

A few miles away, the rain forest commenced, first in tangles of brush, and then gradually thickening to verdant richness. Farther off in the distance, the land undulated upward into lush, forested hills, and beyond that, saw-tooth mountains rose majestically, some of their peaks flecked with snow even at this time of year. The gentlest of breezes wafted across the veranda, the leaves and fronds of the potted plants on the porch quivered with its caress.

Clayton was totally absorbed in the tranquil moment until, for an instant, the faint, disquieting notion crossed his mind that what he was about to do today would spoil all this.

He did not entirely relish the prospect of seeing the man who had an appointment with him today. He had met this reporter socially in London and, in an unguarded moment of generosity, agreed to an interview "sometime," never expecting that the fellow would follow through. Until he called. But no, Clayton concluded, his magazine was lightweight and it would go all right. He dismissed the concern.

The veranda stretched the full width of the two-story wood frame house, a modest villa by European standards but more spacious than any other dwelling in the area. A broad roof spread out over the porch to shield it from the midday sun, and above the roof rose the second story, four gables jutting out at well-spaced intervals. The home was continental in design but complemented by distinctly African touches, such as the use of bamboo, mahogany, and other native woods, as well as the lush flower beds and the stately palm and hardwood trees flanking the yard.

Baaku, his manservant, emerged from the main entrance bearing a dining tray and proceeded to clear the remnants of Clayton's lunch and tidy up.

From around the shrubbery at the side of the house, a monkey came scampering across the yard, chasing something, but suddenly skidded to a stop, pausing while sniffing the air, and looked up at his master and then back out across the landscape.

"Master…," Baaku said, looking up and out over the lawn.

"Yes, I see it."

Off in the distance they watched a cloud of dust made by someone approaching. A moment later, Clayton recognized a Range Rover driving down the road from the northeast. The monkey scampered away toward the rear of the house as the dusty vehicle slowed to turn off the road and pull into the long driveway.

"I will quickly finish cleaning up, sir," said Baaku.

"No, that'll do. Thank you, Baaku," Clayton said to the servant, who withdrew.

Clayton rose and walked forward to stand between the bamboo supporting pillars on either side of the steps leading down to the yard. He calmly watched the vehicle pull up and park. The driver got out, strode across the yard, and climbed halfway up the four wooden steps. He appeared to be in his forties, fashionably dressed in a rather new field jacket with the sleeves rolled up to mid-forearm, cotton trousers crisp, hiking boots barely broken in. Other than his well-barbered light brown hair being somewhat windblown from the ride, he presented the appearance of a clean-cut, urbane reporter who preferred to get his stories from interviews in air-conditioned offices or hotel lounges rather than dusty streets or war-torn cities.

"Lord Greystoke?" he asked, extending his right hand. "Dennis Fletcher, from the *World Chronicle*. It was a bit of a journey getting here. I hope I'm not late."

Clayton reached down to shake his hand and then, and smiling, replied, "Not at all. Right on time."

"Nice place you have here."

"Thank you. Care to look around?"

"Definitely."

They descended the steps and strolled around to the land-scaped yard on the eastern side of the house. "How long have you been here?" Fletcher asked.

"Oh, more than thirty-five years. I lose track of time."

Clayton guided the reporter across the shaded patio and through the manicured grounds. He pointed out the stables and then the garden, where Fletcher noted the straight rows of well-tended flowers and clusters of herbs.

"Very impressive," Fletcher admired. "You seem quite the gardener, Lord Greystoke."

"Not really. I employ one. I have always enjoyed the outdoors, but I've been more of a hunter and traveler than a gardener."

"Are all these beautiful flowers imported?"

"Oh, no. Nearly all are native. That one, for instance." He pointed to a patch of striking yellow flowers in full bloom, their petals the color of golden wheat enfolding bright orange fila-ments. "That's a Ghana daylily. It has remarkable restorative powers. There's a story behind that."

The brief tour moved around to the back of the yard and into the house. Inside, Fletcher regarded the variety of drums scat-tered around the rooms, pausing to tap on a few and listen to their tone. He then moved on to admire the collection of African masks, spears, and bows arranged artfully on the walls, asking, "Are these local?"

"Yes, most of them gifts. Some I made."

Fletcher nodded and looked at his host. "The place is lovely, quite impressive. Thank you for the tour. Shall we get down to business?"

"Certainly," said Clayton. "How about doing this on the porch? Care for iced tea?"

"Love some."

Clayton gestured to Baaku, who had remained unobtrusively nearby, and then led Fletcher out to the veranda.

Taking a seat, Fletcher unslung his leather bag from his shoulder, opened it, and produced a portable cassette recorder, which he set up on the table in front of him. He unwound the black cord from around the plastic microphone, plugged its end into the recorder jack, and propped the microphone up on the table, pointing it across to Clayton. He slipped a new cassette into the recorder and turned to fetch a pen and notebook as he said, "I hope you don't mind. I tape all my interviews. Wouldn't want to get it wrong, would we?" Clayton nodded his assent.

The iced tea arrived in tall, sweating glasses crowned with lemon slices. Fletcher tasted his and nodded approvingly, saying, "I swear, only the British know how to make tea."

The reporter regarded the man who sat in front of him. Lord Greystoke was tall and rugged. A scar of considerable length stretched down across his temple. That, along with various other scars and nicks, suggested that this ostensibly upper-class British gentleman had been through more than a few struggles in his life. Yet, though strands of gray flecked the neatly-clipped hair that must have once been jet black, and a few age lines stretched from around the eyelids and nostrils across his otherwise healthy, tanned skin, this man hardly looked old. His gray eyes were still piercing, his jaw still firm, his voice still resonant, and the short-sleeved, cotton polo shirt he wore hardly concealed the large chest, the firm abdomen, or the still-solid biceps.

Fletcher set his glass down and took up his notebook. "So," he began. "You've been around for a while. In your sixties, I'm guessing? Older?"

"A little older," Clayton said cagily.

"You look well for a man that age. Quite fit. What's your secret, if I may ask?"

Clayton smiled a bemused, noncommittal smile. "I've kept active most of my life. Fresh air, exercise, unadulterated food."

"Now, you inherited your title from your parents, Lord Greystoke and Lady Alice?"

"Yes."

"Where were you born?"

"Here, in Africa."

"When did your parents die?"

"I was quite young."

"But you inherited the family fortune, the Greystoke title. And after seeing England and the continent, and despite your status as a peer of the Realm, you decided to live here."

"For much of the year, yes."

"And your wife?"

"She's in London. She's coming back in three weeks."

"I regret that the timing of my visit did not allow me a chance to chat with her as well. But that brings me to the subject of my article. What do British peers do after they retire? I see for one thing, you've traveled."

"I've traveled to a few countries, such as France and America, but other than in Africa, I've not traveled all that extensively."

"According to the peerage records, you were absent from the House of Lords quite a bit during most of your years there."

"You'll find that many peers are absent a fair amount. The position is an entitlement and doesn't really require much of a commitment. As for me, I had affairs here in Africa which occupied my attention."

"Such as what?"

"Various things," Clayton replied noncommittally. "I've helped some of the tribes with their affairs."

"Oh? Like what?" the reporter pressed.

Clayton put down his glass and reached over to press the stop key on Fletcher's tape recorder. He then sat upright, his gray eyes still able to manage a steely stare, and said, "You're not really doing a story on retired British Peers of the Realm, are you? You could have found at least a half-dozen of them sitting on Hyde Park benches any day of the week. Why did you really come all the way down here?"

Fletcher stiffened slightly and tried to manage a bit of a smile without making it look like a retreat, and said, "Actually, I've come to talk to you about Tarzan."

"Who?"

"Tarzan. The Ape Man. The Lord of the Jungle."

Clayton leaned back to prop his elbows on the arms of his chair and, with fingers interlaced, looked past the reporter's eyes, to the sky. After a moment of silence, he said, "There is no such person. A jungle myth. He does not exist."

"Come, come, we both know better. We both know that you are—or were—Tarzan of the Apes."

Clayton stared blankly at Fletcher, his thin lips firm and close together. "This Tarzan, if he ever existed, is dead."

Fletcher smiled, a bit of condescension showing through. "I've done the research. I've interviewed many people who knew or have come across the ape man over the years. I've traced him here. You really haven't covered your trail all that well, Lord Greystoke."

Clayton took a slow sip of his tea and pondered for a moment. "So you're looking for this Tarzan. If you find him, what do you want with him?"

"I want to ask him what happened."

"What do you mean?"

"Well, we haven't heard from him—from you—for a long time. But this Tarzan was quite the figure in decades past."

"He was?"

"Weren't you involved in the African rebellion against the Nazis when they tried to take over down here in 1938?"

"Oh, did that happen? Was that in the papers?"

"Of course not. Germany denied any such occurrence, and Britain, for whatever reason, kept rather mum about its involvement in the business. But we know from subsequent investigations and post-war interviews that such an incursion did take place and was put down. By you."

"The Africans resisted and defeated them."

"Led by you," Fletcher pressed.

"I was of some assistance, yes. But I could hardly do that sort of thing alone."

"That's not all. You've rescued expeditions; you've saved dozens, maybe hundreds, of lives. I have accounts of you performing feats of strength and endurance that rival those of Olympic athletes. By some accounts, even talking to animals."

Clayton took a deep breath, his massive chest swelling and then relaxing. He stirred the ice in his glass absent-mindedly for a moment and then looked directly into the reporter's gaze. "All right. Yes. I am who you say I am. Or was. But I haven't done such things for a long time. It's all past now. I'd like to live out the latter days of my life in peace, if you don't mind."

"Oh, I'm not here to change that," Fletcher smiled. "My article will be, if anything, a tribute. I'd just like to know it all—the whole story of the life of one of the most incredible figures of our time."

The corners of Clayton's thin lips curled slightly upward. "The whole story? Well, Mr. Fletcher, the whole story, as you put it, is much more extensive than you could fit into one article, and I doubt that your readers would even believe most of it. But I could tell you stories, yes. I could tell you about being raised among apes, having not even a clue about my language or my heritage until I was nearly a teenager. I could tell you about visiting lost tribes in ancient cities, like one whose inhabitants were ape-like men and incredibly beautiful women and whose underground chambers contained vast stores of treasure. I could tell you about visiting another long-lost civilization where the inhabitants still live the way they did in ancient Rome, or one where the inhabitants still live in the Middle Ages, complete with knights in armor." Clayton took a slow, measured sip of his tea, as if he were merely recalling a grocery list, and added, "How many days do you have?"

Fletcher arched his eyebrows and replied, "Are you kidding?" with the seasoned-journalist's equivalent of the expression of a child beholding a huge ice cream cone. "My schedule is open! I only hope I have enough batteries!"

Clayton settled back in his chair and paused for a moment, as if to collect his thoughts. Then he began, "My father was John Clayton, Lord Greystoke of London. His wife, my mother, was the former Alice Rutherford. He had been assigned a mission to investigate claims of slaving in British West African colonies, and he took her along. She was pregnant, which, as you might expect, might not have been the best idea."

"And you were born en route?" Fletcher asked.

"The sailors aboard their vessel mutinied, and they were set ashore, in the jungles of West Africa, to fend for themselves. I was born soon after, in a cabin my father built, and then subsequently my mother and then my father perished. I was alone."

"But then how did you manage—" Fletcher began, but was cut off.

"Master! Look!" the servant Baaku interrupted, pointing out across the front yard.

Heading down the long driveway was a rusted sedan whose finish had long been tarnished by the sun. As it rolled down the driveway toward the estate, it churned up more of a cloud of dust than the reporter had, evidently in much more of a hurry.

The driver got out and ran up to the veranda and stopped at the bottom of the steps, looking up to Clayton. Fletcher saw that he was an African man, perhaps in his early twenties, his face and torso dripping with sweat that soaked through his loosely fitting, coarse shirt. He also wore dark short pants, and his feet were shod in dusty canvas sandals.

"Lord Greystoke," he said breathlessly. "Baaku's family! A wire! From Kaltu. There is a…a matter in their village." He paused to cough and clutch his chest.

Both Clayton and Baaku knew that his use of the term "matter" was a euphemism for "trouble," a concession to the presence of the outsider Fletcher.

"Kaltu is the closest town, about ten miles from here," Clayton explained to the reporter. "This man is Waziri, which is Baaku's tribe, and my adopted tribe. He says his home village has sent a wire to Kaltu and he has come to relay it to Baaku. And to me."

"His family has sent a wire to you? Why didn't they just call? I noticed a telephone in your parlor."

"Because they do not have a telephone. Most of the people in his village do not. In case you hadn't noticed, we are not exactly in the Cotswolds, Mr. Fletcher." Turning to Baaku, he said, "Give him food and drink. And then close up. We must make preparations."

"What are you going to do?" asked Fletcher.

"We will journey to the Waziri home village of Kumali and see what has happened. They may need help. Our interview is over, I'm afraid."

"Well, how about if I tag along?" Fletcher asked.

"This is a private matter," Clayton said flatly. "It does not concern you."

"Everything concerns me. I'm a reporter. There may be a story in it. And I may be of assistance. I have connections. We can take my vehicle."

"It might be dangerous," Clayton said.

"I'll take the risk," Fletcher asserted. "You're not responsible for me."

"I most certainly am not."

Chapter 2

THE WAZIRI

Dennis Fletcher's Range Rover careened over rutted roads that snaked through grassland and veldt before merging onto more paved roads as he and Clayton neared the town of Kumali. Baaku and the messenger followed them in the messenger's sedan.

The ride was uneventful. Clayton said little for long stretches, save for occasionally giving directions where to turn. At length, the reporter, used to making his living by conversation, needed to break the silence.

"Is it always this hot?"

"No, it often gets hotter."

"How much farther?"

"Another ten or fifteen miles," Clayton replied. "I've never measured it by road."

"Where are we going, exactly?"

"To Kumali, the village where most of the Waziri live."

"Who are these Waziri, besides Baaku's people?"

"They are one of the great tribes of this area. Until two generations ago, the Waziri lived as their forefathers had for a thousand years, in the jungle. They hunted and fished and cultivated the land. They made their own huts and clothing and tools. They had villages in their own territory, and they were self-sufficient on it. Now all that is changed."

"Why?"

"Colonization, progress, corporate greed, call it what you will. First came the European explorers and hunters slaughtering the wildlife. And trying to civilize the natives. Then came the lumber and chemical and rubber and mining companies. Little by little, the tribes lost or sold their lands, and now they live in buildings, in towns. But under the surface they are still a warrior people, a noble race. The older ones teach the Waziri language and ways to the younger ones."

"But isn't progress better?"

"I don't know. You tell me when we get there."

As they passed through expanses of field and scrub trees bordering the road, the land became more forested. "Look over there," said Clayton, pointing toward huge diesel bulldozers and tractors. They heard the roar of buzz and chain saws in a logging operation. "That is what you should be writing about," he said.

"What, cutting down trees?" asked Fletcher.

"That used to be a huge, primitive forest," Clayton explained. "Great trees a hundred, two hundred years old. Now they are all being clear cut. Sometimes hundreds of acres. More every day. The entire African landscape is changing. Greedy white Europeans and Americans have come in and bought, swindled, or stolen the land. They destroy wildlife habitats and hunting grounds, change the direction of rivers, whatever they want. Tribal lands that were hunted and fished for a thousand years are being parceled out like so many commodities."

"Interesting," Fletcher said, somewhat noncommittally. "I hadn't realized."

"The story here is not my past," Clayton added. "The story here is Africa's future."

They entered the outer limits of the town of Kumali. They first passed ramshackle huts encircling the perimeter and, farther in, brick facades of the central town. Clayton directed Fletcher to drive through several downtown streets, some paved and some dusty, until they arrived in a residential area consisting of many small streets jutting off the main one. Clustered on these side streets were rows of one-story wood houses, simple and boxy but neat, with modest yards, often nestled among shrubs and trees. An expanse of jungle began not far from many of the yards, seemingly held at bay by the edges of the town.

Word had evidently circulated about their arrival, so that by the time Fletcher pulled up the vehicle and parked, a delegation of about a dozen men and women had assembled to meet them. Most of the men were middle-aged, but a few had grayer heads. Though they were dressed in colorful robes, dashikis, and head wraps, their stance was dignified and somber. The women seemed more troubled, but they, too, were restrained.

When Clayton got out of the passenger door, the grim faces of several of the Africans broke into grins as they greeted him. Fletcher saw smiles and handshakes all around, as if they were greeting an old friend.

Clayton turned to the reporter to say, "These are some of the Waziri. This is their village." Clayton indicated a handsome, muscular, firm-jawed man at the head of the delegation and said, "Let me introduce Dajan. He is the chief. I have known him since he was a boy." Fletcher observed the man who smiled and shook his hand to be about fifty, a few inches shorter than Clayton, dressed in an elegant dashiki and matching headcloth and sporting a necklace of—could he be right about this?— animal teeth. The other Waziri men were similarly garbed in loose-fitting African robes, displaying copper bracelets or anklets and sometimes medallions with intricate metal or bead work. All the Waziri carried themselves proudly, with dignity, the reporter noted.

"What is the trouble?" Clayton asked. He addressed them in their language—purposely, Fletcher reckoned, so that he would not be able to follow.

Several men blurted out replies at once, each trying to talk over the other.

Fletcher knew a smattering of Swahili, and the Waziri tongue was similar enough to Swahili that Fletcher understood some of them to be saying, "Obutu was here."

"Obutu?" Fletcher asked.

Clayton said, "You've heard of Sefu Abadd, who was the ruler of several provinces in this territory for years?"

Fletcher nodded.

Clayton continued, "Well, Abadd's general, a man named Obutu, took over and proclaimed himself ruler about six months ago."

"Ah, yes. His government, if you can call it that, has been giving some of us a devil of a time with visas and entrance requirements. Essentially a military dictator, isn't he?"

"You could say that. Obutu's experience was being in charge of the army and the secret police. Let's say diplomacy and the finer arts of governance are not his strong suit."

Clayton turned and continued to converse with the Waziri in their language. Several of them gestured animatedly, and some of the women became teary-eyed. After a few exchanges, he turned to Fletcher and said rather flatly, with just a bit of a forced courtesy smile, "I'm afraid the nature of this problem means that our interview is over for today, Mr. Fletcher. We'll have to continue another time. Thank you for the ride. There is some pressing tribal business to attend to right now, and the Waziri do not care for a reporter being present. You may refuel your vehicle downtown. The road that will take you to Lumbazo is that way. I believe that's where you said your hotel is?"

"Yes," Fletcher said. "When can we continue the interview? We hardly got started."

"Perhaps when I'm finished here. I'll call you."

Disappointed at the turn of events, and not a little put off, Dennis Fletcher secured his equipment in the back of his vehicle and drove off, heading north out of town. The seasoned reporter was familiar enough with the "brush-off" and not one to give up readily. At this point, however, he could not be certain where his real story, and thus his real interest, lay. On the one hand, as Clayton had earlier intimated, a story might be found here with the tribes, which meant that Fletcher should devote his efforts to poking around Kumali and its environs to see what was going on. On the other hand, his original purpose had been to produce an in-depth profile of John Clayton, Lord Greystoke, in all his incarnations, and he felt that if he were ever to realize that goal, he ought to respect the wishes of his subject, go back to his hotel, and hope for another opportunity later.

WHILE FLETCHER MULLED OVER the events of the day, Clayton and at least two dozen Waziri tribesmen gathered around a large Formica-topped table in their central meeting hall.

"He took our children!" several of them said, nearly at once.

"What?" replied the astonished Clayton.

Dajan explained, "Obutu drove right into town with three trucks full of armed soldiers. They got out and went from house to house, grabbing every child they could find, and herding them onto a truck. The soldiers fired shots, but only at the air. I think they had orders not to kill anyone."

"Maybe that would have been preferable to this," said Komboa, an angry father of two.

"The mothers and grandmothers screamed, clinging to the children as the soldiers pulled them away," said Mwanga, one of the elders. "Some of us resisted, of course. But they knocked us down and held machine guns to us. We had to just stand there and grit our teeth, helpless, or be shot down while we watched them load our children into their trucks. They ransacked our houses and confiscated all our rifles, too. They left the spears and bows, thinking, I suppose, that those were no threat."

"Did they take all the children?" Clayton asked.

"They didn't take the time to grab them all. Some were hiding, or out in the woods, and they left the infants and the very small ones. But they rounded up at least thirty."

His brow furrowed, Clayton asked, "What did he want with them?"

"He said his needs were simple," Dajan replied. "He needed money."

"Why?"

"To equip his army," said Mwanga. "He says he is the future of Africa and he invited us to join in the movement and share in the glory."

"By taking our children!?" exclaimed Komboa angrily.

"He said every village in the province will be required to contribute to the new government, and this will be our contribution," said another tribesman, with a scowl. "He said we should feel fortunate because all he wants from us is money. The villages which do not have money will have to contribute their sons."

"He said he would return them safe and unharmed if we do what he wanted," Dajan added.

"And what is that?" Clayton asked.

"He says he has been told that we have a source of gold."

"How does he know about that?" one of the men grumbled.

"It does not matter!" Komboa shot back. "He knows! He told us not to bother denying it."

Dajan continued, "He knows that we can get gold. He told us to present him with three hundred thousand British pounds in gold if we want our children returned. He gave us two months. He said if we do not have it by then, he will kill one child per day until we do."

Clayton breathed out a pensive sigh and stared at the tabletop as he momentarily contemplated the implications of what had happened. Then he raised his head, jutted out his chin, and said, "We cannot let him harm the children. But we also cannot rescue them. If we did, there would be retaliation. We are no match for Obutu's military forces."

"What are we going to do?" asked Matu, a tribesman at the end of the table.

"There is only one thing we can do," another tribesman said. "We must give him what he wants."

"But that means…" Matu's voice trailed off.

"Yes," Clayton said. "We know what it means." He looked around the room, one by one, at the eyes of the Waziri tribesmen. In all of them, he read the assent and the steely determination that would be necessary for the task ahead.

After a silent moment, he said, "It means we must go to Opar."

Chapter 3

DETOUR

Dennis Fletcher headed out the crudely-paved gravel road north of Kumali and drove for about five miles, where he joined a wider, more well-paved road that would lead him to Lumbazo about thirty-five more miles away. He soon passed beyond the thicker jungle and cruised past open, grassy plains. The road was sparsely traveled and the way ahead was clear, so that he felt he could lean on the pedal a bit, driving slowly enough to watch for animal crossings but fast enough to make some time.

He pondered what to do next about the elusive Lord Greystoke. He knew something of the exploits of the legendary Tarzan of the Apes from his research, but after meeting the hospitable though rather taciturn lord in person, he was convinced that there must be much more beneath the surface. He considered his options, such as when to call him from his hotel to resume the interview. He also wondered whether, if Lord Greystoke were to be detained at Kumali for some time, he should hire a translator and just go back there. After all, Fletcher reasoned in true journalistic mode, the subject did agree to an interview, and his editor would not wait forever.

The road took him past long stretches of lush green forests interrupted now and again by patches of open plains. It had not all been cut down yet, the reporter noted. There were still many square miles of essentially untouched jungle and broad, golden veldts.

Beautiful country, he thought. I can see why somebody might choose to give up smoggy London to live here.

About two miles from Lumbazo, he came upon a roadblock. Stretched across the road was a painted yellow barricade supported by triangular wooden stands on either side. Two uniformed guards, a large burly one and a younger, leaner one, stood at the barricade with brandished rifles. The burly one waved to him to stop as he approached.

As he braked to a halt, the soldiers walked forward and took up a position on either side of the vehicle. Fletcher looked from one to the other, apprehensive but trying to look composed. The guard on the driver's side, the burly one, approached Fletcher's open window and said in East-African-accented English, "Turn off the engine." Fletcher complied.

"Where are you going?"

"I'm going to Lumbazo. To my hotel there. Is there a problem?"

"Let me see your passport."

From his breast pocket Fletcher produced his passport, which the guard looked over, as if he were searching for some particular item of information.

"Fel...Fletcher...?" the guard stumbled through his name. "What are you doing here in the country of General Obutu?"

"I'm a reporter. I'm on assignment."

"Reporter?" The guard seemed either interested or bemused, as if he did not believe Fletcher. "What do you write?"

"I work for the *World Chronicle*. We report on world events, travel, cuisine, personalities...perhaps you've heard of it?"

The guard mumbled gruffly, putting the passport in his pocket. He then proceeded to push his rifle through the open back window of the vehicle and poke around among Fletcher's possessions. With a nod from the first guard, the second opened the rear door on the other side of the vehicle and reached in.

"Hey," Fletcher said. "My passport! And leave that stuff alone." The burly man leveled his rifle rather ominously six inches from Fletcher's face, which quickly silenced him.

The younger one picked up a small black case about the size of a briefcase and said, "What is this?"

"Typewriter," Fletcher said. "You know, tool of the trade…?"

The guard undid the latch and opened the top to look briefly at the portable Smith-Corona and then closed it and returned it to the seat. He then picked up Fetcher's camera bag and began pawing through it.

"Leave my camera alone!" Fletcher protested.

After apparently satisfying his curiosity about what it was, the guard replaced the camera equipment in the bag and tossed it onto the back seat. He took a few more moments to rummage through the remainder of Fletcher's things, including his valise and tape recorder bag. He then looked up at the guard holding the rifle in Fletcher's face and nodded, saying, "Reporter."

The burly guard stepped back and gestured with his weapon for Fletcher to get out of the vehicle, saying, "You will come with us."

"What!?" Fletcher protested.

"Come with us to Lumbazo. You may get to meet His Excellency!"

"Come with us to Lumbazo. You may get to meet His Excellency!"

Chapter 4

THE EXPEDITION

Opar.

It was the darkest of Africa's many dark secrets, the ancient, long-lost city hidden deep in the bowels of the continent.

Clayton had first journeyed to the city decades ago, having heard tales about a lost city from the son of an old Waziri chieftain.

Its origins were mysterious, shrouded in antiquity. Archeologists would have a field day unlocking its secrets. There was even some evidence suggesting that its structures might date back to the lost Atlantis. No one ever knew.

When Clayton found it, the stone walls and buildings and parapets had already begun to crumble. Its main edifice had clearly once been a magnificent temple. In its center lay a massive stone slab whose rusty crimson stains suggested human sacrifices had long been staged there.

The city was as much fortress as temple. Its walls and towers were clearly designed to resist attackers. To that end, no looming gate or entranceway opened through the main wall, but only a small cleft so narrow that Clayton had had to turn nearly sideways to enter. Beneath the temple lay a network of tunnels and many levels of prison cells and animal cages.

Clayton had found the city inhabited by a curious race of brutish, half-human men and, inexplicably, beautiful women, including their high priestess, La. But these people might not have been the original inhabitants of the city. There was no

21

reason to believe that they did not also discover it themselves and might have been merely part of a long succession of dwellers. Now even they had disappeared, so that for years Opar had been a dead city. The true architects of Opar were so long buried that their identities will always remain yet another of the great mysteries of the Dark Continent.

The most incredible feature of this remarkable place, however, was its gold. The original builders of the city had evidently found massive deposits of the metal somewhere, for it generously embellished their spires and minarets. They used it in the trim of their walls and doorways, in the gilt of their ornate scrollwork, and even in the decorative patterns of their streets. Moreover, Clayton had discovered huge stores of gold bars in vaults deep beneath the streets of Opar. He did not believe that the most recent occupants of the city even knew the value of the precious metal, apart from its beauty and malleability. Given their seclusion, they evidently had not traded with other tribes.

Clayton had been there a half dozen times over the decades, and his life had been in jeopardy there more than once. He had been imprisoned in its dank cells and nearly sacrificed twice on its stone altar.

Despite all the perils of his earlier journeys to Opar, Clayton returned to the ruins repeatedly for its gold. No one else, as far as he could determine, had ever discovered the city and its treasures. It was literally there for the taking. He did not deplete the gold supply and try to haul it all out. When he led the last several expeditions to the city, he brought about fifty Waziri warriors, each equipped with a specially-made harness to allow him to carry two ingots on his back, which was all that even a fit and well-muscled warrior could carry and retain the strength and agility necessary for the return trip. This periodic loss of a hundred-odd ingots barely diminished the cache in the vaults.

The Opar riches were never squandered by Clayton and the Waziri. Judiciously used, they paid for housing improvements, for the purchase of tools and equipment, and for the European education of any Waziri child who wished one. They fashioned some of the gold into modest jewelry, but the tribe strove zealously to avoid conspicuous consumption. Indeed, the last thing the Waziri wanted was to present the appearance of windfall wealth. If the tribe should suddenly be observed living a far more luxurious lifestyle than neighboring tribes, especially in these uncertain times, undesirable suspicion would be aroused.

And so it was that when General Obutu chose to demand money of the tribe, rather than some other recompense, Clayton's and the tribe's reaction was not so much astonishment at the amount, but rather worry as to how he had come to believe that they could afford such a sum.

"Does he know about the city?" Mwanga asked.

"He must. Or else he would not demand so much," Dajan reasoned.

"Maybe he just thinks we are a wealthy tribe," one of the tribesmen essayed.

"If he thought that, he would not have given us two months," Dajan retorted. "He knows we have to journey to get it."

"It's clear that he does not know the location of the city, or else he would go there himself," Clayton surmised.

"But how could he know about the city at all?" Mwanga asked.

"For years, he was head of the secret police," said another tribesman. "It was his job to know things."

"It does not matter how," Dajan replied. "He knows. And he has our children. We have no choice now but to pay." Dajan drew a somber breath and added, "And that means we must journey once again to Opar, as our fathers did." He turned to look at Clayton and added, "With Tarzan of the Apes."

At these words, the others looked at Clayton, too. He had not been addressed by that title in some time, but it was the fitting appellation to use, for it would not be Lord Greystoke, English nobleman, who would lead them to the lost city. They needed the Lord of the Jungle, their longtime ally and honorary chief, to whom they had long ago pledged their loyalty.

Dajan looked into the still-bright gray eyes of the noble lord, sought a clue to his reaction from the lined but still robust visage. Though he did not give voice to them, Dajan's look asked many questions: Are you fit? Can you handle the strain? Will you help us one more time?

For his part, Clayton had no hesitancy. He would do what he had to do for the tribe which had come to his aid and rescue time and again. "Then we must go," he said. "We must plan and equip an expedition. Select as many able-bodied men as you can spare. We must prepare quickly and we must leave without drawing attention to what we are doing or where we are going."

And thus it was decided. One day was all that the Waziri needed to equip their expedition. Forty men were selected. The number was an uneasy compromise between the many who wanted to go and the ones who were required to stay to provide services necessary to run the village. They had to give the appearance of normalcy and throw off suspicion that anything was different. Clayton thought the number sufficient to bring back more than enough gold, though he would have preferred fifty.

Back at his villa, Clayton shed his cotton polo shirt and pleated trousers, for on this journey there would be no suitcase or toiletries, no wallet or passport. Like the others, he would wear only an animal skin loin cloth, and he would carry only the weapons he took down from his walls—a great hand-crafted bow, an antelope-hide quiver of arrows, and a keen, well-balanced hunting knife in a hand-tooled sheath and belt.

He left Baaku and his other servants in charge of the villa and returned to Kumali before nightfall the next day, to share in the brief ceremony of well-wishing. Clayton recalled how in times past when an expedition left, the Waziri sent it off with a great feast including drumming and dancing around a roaring bonfire. But such were the times and the nature of this mission that a subdued farewell ceremony was all that could be risked.

BY THE TIME THE VILLAGE AROSE for the day, the expedition was miles away, disappearing into the dense jungle that began a few miles outside of Kumali.

They maintained a brisk pace, Clayton and Dajan in the lead followed by the tribesmen in a column two or three abreast. Each man bore a full array of weapons including bow and quiver, sturdy spear, and hunting knife. In addition, they brought along a modicum of medical supplies, materials and spare weapons carried in hide satchels upon hammocks stretched between two poles that pairs of men bore on their shoulders. They took little food beyond a few trail rations, because these skilled woodsmen would hunt as they went.

To an outside observer, the sight of an older and nearly naked white man walking side by side with clean-limbed, ebony African tribesmen might have seemed strange, but it was of no matter to the Waziri. Rather, they were honored to be in the company of the man who had achieved the status of a legend in their tribal lore. It had been years since any Waziri had hunted or explored with the white lord, and at least half the men in the company were young enough never to have been afield or in battle with him at all. Only a handful of them besides Dajan had ever been to Opar. But tribal memories are long, and they had all grown up enthralled with the stories of the lost city and the exploits of their ally. Thus, not a single Waziri felt the least qualm about following Lord Greystoke wherever the mission might take them. He was one of them in every sense. He was Tarzan of the Apes, transformed mentally as well as physically from a staid English peer to a noble, primitive jungle warrior, a transformation that had always been as easy for Clayton as donning a loin cloth and setting foot in the jungle. It did not matter that he had not been out in the wilderness for a while. He maintained as brisk a pace as the ablest of the

Waziri, hour after hour, his endurance undiminished by his age. Indeed, he wished that he could take to the trees and travel more rapidly through the jungle in the manner in which he was raised by the great apes.

THE JOURNEY TO OPAR was long and arduous. It involved a trek of many days through dense, primitive jungle, with all of the challenges to survival that entailed. It involved following one of the great African rivers westward toward its source, then across a low divide to meet and follow another river. It involved scaling a barricade of craggy hills with treacherous slopes and descending the other side to a broad, barren valley strewn with boulders, and finally squeezing their way through a narrow pass between two great rocky escarpments until they reached the towers and spires of the hidden city.

The way was known only to the ape man and the handful of older Waziri who had been there before. They followed no map, since Tarzan had never drawn one, lest it fall into the wrong hands. As with each previous expedition, the ones who knew the way schooled the others on the distinctive landmarks and the geography of the route so that any one of them could lead the next expedition, should the need arise.

The route took less time than it used to because in subsequent expeditions they had discovered shortcuts and grown more efficient in traversing the landscape. Yet they traveled long days, from sunup to sundown. They were sustained during the day by wild berries and fruits they found on the way and by jerky and a type of fried dough they had brought along. At night, they ate well, feasting on roasted fresh kills enriched by fragrant herbs they had also brought with them, though, regrettably, they could bring none of their native beer.

Oral tradition was strong in the Waziri tribe, and around the nightly campfires the time between supper and sleep was filled with laughter and camaraderie and talk of the exploits and battles of the tribe and their ape man ally, not the least of which were the tales of Tarzan in the fabled lost city. Stories were told—indeed, dramatically narrated—about Tarzan and renegade Arabs, about tribal wars, about battling Nazis bent on conquest, about the many times the tribe and the ape man had aided, and often rescued, each other, all for the gratification of the older ones and edification of the younger.

Though the tribesmen had gone out on jungle expeditions even after settling down to life in Kumali, it had been a long time since one like this. Despite the grimness of their purpose, their fraternal bonds were strong and their amicability high. The jungle had been the tribal home to this warrior race for so many generations that it was still second nature to them, still in their veins, as indeed it still was to Tarzan of the Apes.

Chapter 5

THE PEACE CORPS

From the journal of Eric Benton, November 2:
>   *We're celebrating our one month anniversary at Tswana today. We're breaking out the beer, and Cathie made a cake because we were able to score some extra sugar on our last supply shipment.*

>   *Wow, a month already!*

>   *In the past month, I've done more than I expected I ever would or could. I lived for three weeks without running water or electricity or television. I tasted roast antelope and stewed water buffalo. I've worked with our native partners, and even though they speak some English, they jovially made me speak only their Swahili dialect for a whole day at a time, and I did!*

>   *I remember writing that I wanted to help people, and I really think I have. I've seen the smiles on the faces of the African villagers as they show their gratitude for the things we've been doing.*

>   *As a BA generalist, I don't have all the technical know-how, but I assisted in the building of a school and in digging their new well. The Corps also built a small hospital in the area and began vaccinations for typhoid.*

>   *And I became good friends with some of the most interesting people I ever met. They come from all parts of the country. There's our Fearless Leader, Scott Gordon, who is 35 and has been in the Corps for eight years and in three countries. He's our Assistant Country Director for the district (AD for short). He's an inspiration every day. He*

*knows the ins and outs in Washington and he can get things
we need, like a generator and decent medical supplies and,
yes, beer. He comes by and checks on our progress from time
to time, and he made sure he would be on hand today.*

*The others are all great. Some of them are on staggered
tours of duty working in other villages, and we cross paths
from time to time, like Lex Cooper, a good ol' farm boy from
Minnesota, and Jeff Barker, who is in pre-med. They're
here today, too.*

*I work at the village with Todd Fitzgerald, an engi-
neering graduate who is amazing. I've been doing a lot of
the grunt work helping these guys, and I sure learned a lot.*

*Our girls are great, too. Cathie Burnette from Oregon
teaches the village kids elementary English and is a whiz
at repairing our clothes. And, of course, then there's Judy
Malone who has really made this experience worth it for
me. More on her later!*

Six days after Dennis Fletcher visited the Greystoke villa,
Eric Benton and his Peace Corps co-workers were in the midst
of celebrating the one-month anniversary of their work in
Africa. Their encampment was a series of semi-permanent
plywood huts adjacent to Tswana, a small, poverty-stricken
village that the Peace Corps had selected because of its high
infant mortality rate, its substandard housing, its lack of sanita-
tion, and its generally dire need of aid. Their celebration coin-
cided with the completion of a new well, so that the village
could enjoy fresh water and quite probably cut its disease rate.

Inside their central "mess hut," the soaring voice of Grace
Slick on "Somebody to Love" wailed out of a small, secondhand
guitar amp in the corner, patched from Eric's cassette deck.
The heads of the volunteers bobbed to the music, and laughter
rippled underneath it. Out back, Lex Cooper, the wiry, red-
faced farm boy, tended to sausages sizzling on a makeshift grill
fashioned from an oil drum, the pungent, satisfying smoke
permeating the air.

Todd Fitzgerald and Cathie Burnette were dancing. Todd, twenty-four, was tall and lanky, with curly brown hair. He had spent the last two weeks laboring over the design of the well and latrine and was relieved to be able to kick back and take his mind off work for an afternoon. Cathie, twenty-eight, bounced rhythmically to the music with a broad grin, occasionally pushing her spectacles back on her nose or adjusting her hat that she needed to protect her freckled skin.

On this day off, most of the young Corps volunteers wore open shirts over tank tops or T-shirts with cutoff shorts or jeans and hiking boots. The well-trimmed haircut Eric's father had always insisted upon in Oshkosh had grown rather shaggy. Though Eric still shaved daily, several of the young men, most notably Jeff, had allowed their beards to grow.

They passed around bottles of Tusker beer, cooled nicely by the refrigerator their generator had powered for the past three hours.

A few African children of the village stood near the doorway to the shelter, sporting wide, toothy grins and weaving to the beat of the music. They had been promised cake and were eagerly awaiting it.

Though thankful for their aid, the residents of this small village had been a bit put off at first by the denimed appearance of this motley group from America. But in the past month they had grown very grateful for the young people's diligence and cheerful demeanor, and come to accept them as part of the village life, though they still thought that their music was a little strange.

A few villagers had stopped by, chatting with the Corps youth, and left a tray of local fruit to complement the potato chips and other snacks on the camp dining table near the center of the shelter. Judy Malone's green eyes sparkled with a cheery "Thanks!"

Eric, sitting cross-legged on the floor next to the fridge, said, "Let's do this every month!" to Scott Gordon, who was walking by.

Scott, the senior supervisor in the area, smiled and replied, "We were lucky we could get a few extra things on the shipment. Maybe again in six months." The laugh lines around his pale blue eyes wrinkled as he smiled.

Despite his thinning hair and the wrinkles on his sun-burnished face, Scott rarely frowned and retained that youthful optimism that kept his younger charges energized through their often arduous tasks. His most common statement was an enthusiastic "Yes, you can!" which became the rallying cry of the Corps members in his charge.

"How about this, eh?" said Lex, popping open his bottle of beer with his church key. "Almost as good as Pabst! Great weather, beer, good eats, good friends. Not bad for the middle of nowhere!"

"The only thing missing is a joint!" said Jeff, his long, straggly black hair nearly covering one eye as it hung down over his brow.

"Shhh!" Lex said, chortling. "We'll get in trouble!"

Eric smiled non-committally but wondered what his straight-arrow father would say.

The Corps volunteers spent a certain amount of time congratulating and complimenting each other on the work that they had done in the villages, but mostly the conversation was about home and family.

"I almost didn't come," said Jeff, "because my girl didn't want me to leave…." His voice drifted off as if he were remembering conversations he would rather not repeat. He then turned to Eric and asked, "So, you regret coming here?"

"No, not yet," Eric smiled.

Changing the subject, Jeff grinned and said, "Why don't you ask Judy to dance? You know you want to."

They both looked toward Judy, who was cutting and arrang-
ing pieces of cake at the dining table. Eric looked for an instant
at the way her straight brown hair cascaded around her shoulders and the way her tanned arm flexed as she worked the knife.

"What do you mean?"

"You know what I mean. You've been eyeing her for a while."

"I have?"

"Don't deny it. It shows."

"How bad? Think she can tell?"

"Only one way to find out. Go over there. Go on," Jeff
coaxed, and then added with a grin, "I promised I'd be faithful
to Trudy."

As Barker got up to get another beer, Eric seized the moment
to wander over to Judy. "Nice job cutting the cake," was all he
could think of to say.

"Thanks," Judy smiled, licking frosting off her slim finger.
"It's nice to have some time off."

"Yeah," Eric replied, and then added, "Uh…wanna dance a
little?"

Judy smiled her wide, green-eyed smile and agreed. They
stepped a few feet away from the snack table and toward the
speaker and began to gyrate to a modified Twist.

The song would end in a minute, and Eric remembered that
he had put "Cherish" next on the compilation tape. He just
began to weigh the chances of her staying there with him long
enough for that honey-sweet song to start and give him a shot
at a slow dance, when they heard a commotion outside. At first
it sounded like the pop of firecrackers, but it was quickly followed by the screaming of some village women. Then some
men shouted. Scott ran to the doorway, looked out, and cried,
"Soldiers! They're shooting!" They all threw down their beer
and soda cans and rushed to the doorway to see.

Three huge, rumbling khaki-colored military transport trucks
had just roared into the village. Uniformed soldiers leaning
out from the sides of two of them were firing bursts from assault

rifles. The trucks pulled in and braked to a stop near the village center. Women screamed and scooped up their children who had been playing in the street.

Chaos broke out. In an instant, a cacophony of screams and shouts mingled with curses and barked orders as armed African soldiers poured out of two of the trucks and spread out, many of them firing shots into the air. Panicking, the villagers scattered in turmoil.

The soldiers pursued the scrambling villagers down the streets and alleys. At one house after another, soldiers burst in and came out pulling boys or young men by the arm and hauling them to the backs of the transport trucks, where other soldiers forced them inside at gunpoint.

Some resisted, only to be struck across the face or back with rifle stocks. One young man broke free from his captor and took off. A moment later he was shot in the leg as he ran, and he fell to the dirt. His father, enraged, ran cursing toward one of the soldiers, but was stopped in his tracks by a soldier's bullet fired into the dirt barely a foot from him.

In the space of a few minutes, at least a dozen young men and boys were rounded up and herded onto the truck. Most were between fifteen and twenty years old. A few of the boys were as young as ten or eleven. Several mothers fell to their knees in the dirt, wailing and crying. Men stood on the side of the road near their houses, shouting their anger, some shaking their fists.

After the young men had been seized, at least a dozen soldiers moved out from the trucks and formed two half circles on either side of each parked truck. They leveled their weapons at the crowd, and the villagers quieted down, so that after a moment only unspoken tension mingled with the acrid mixture of gunsmoke and upchurned dust that hung in the air.

A large, stocky man in uniform got out of the largest vehicle and strode forward toward the assembled crowd, his broad shoulders and wide hips swaying as he walked, giving him a distinctive swagger. He stopped about ten feet from the largest cluster of villagers and stood for a moment, allowing them all to drink in his magnificence. If he heard the sound of crying infants in the distance, he ignored it.

"I am General Obutu," he said grandly, in their dialect. "If you do not know me, you will."

General Obutu stood about five-foot-eight, yet must have weighed more than two-hundred-thirty pounds. Beneath the visor of his military cap, his deep black face, broad and glistening with perspiration, was marked by a wide forehead, ample cheekbones, and flared nostrils. His full-lipped mouth might have been capable of a hearty grin, but coupled with his firm brow, it produced today a pronounced scowl. The general was dressed in a brown military uniform trimmed with crimson. Over a khaki shirt and Windsor-knotted necktie, he wore a military waist jacket with brass-buttoned shoulder epaulets. The front of the jacket was resplendent with ribbons and insignia and medals of silver and brass.

About his waist was strapped a .45 automatic pistol secured in a smart leather holster with flap. His creased trousers were expertly tucked into and folded over the tops of black leather boots that were well polished, a considerable feat in this dusty area. Strapped to his calf was a small dagger in a black leather sheath. His ensemble was completed with, inexplicably, a riding crop. Since there were clearly no horses in the area, Eric wondered whether he felt the need to swat his vehicle driver from time to time.

The general paused for effect, looking slowly back and forth from face to face in the crowd.

"I am here to save your country. Our country," he said. "We Africans must continue to throw off the yoke of the European oppressors and determine our own future. I am here to help you do that. My movement can be your salvation, your hope for the future. But in order to fulfill my destiny, the destiny of the African people, I need your help."

"You are going to take our children!?" one distraught father shouted.

Obutu smiled condescendingly and said, "You do not understand. This is your way to contribute to the liberation of your country. I need your sons for my army. They will serve their country, their people. They are cowering boys now, but I will make them soldiers. They will make you proud."

Obutu spun on his heels and gestured to his brigade. The last of the anxious young men were immediately herded into one of the waiting transport trucks. Mothers and grandmothers screamed and wailed, their arms extended in pleading. Some of the men spat curses through clenched teeth. The semicircle of General Obutu's soldiers tightened their grips on their machine guns and rifles. They dug their heels in, standing firmly, scanning the crowd for any untoward movements.

Would they actually shoot the villagers? Eric wondered.

After the young men of the village had been secured in the truck, Obutu strode slowly down the rows of villagers who, incensed as they were, held back their rage. He stared at them one by one, almost daring them to make a move. None did. His impassive face registered no emotion, but his manner had an air of disappointment that this abduction had been so easily done. Clearly, he was looking for a way to present a more impressive display of his power.

In exchanged whispers, the Americans checked to ascertain whether they had all understood what was being said. A moment before he was ready to leave, General Obutu noticed the Peace Corps encampment at the end of the road and heard snatches of the conversation. He strode over to the shelter where the volunteers had been partying not fifteen minutes earlier and faced the group of shaggy-haired white faces nervously watching him.

"Who are you?" Obutu asked, in English.

"We are Americans," said Scott. "Peace Corps."

"Why are you here?"

"We have been sent by our country to help these villagers."

"I need your sons for my army!"

"Indeed?" the general said with a smile. He strode like a peacock over to where the meat was grilling, now smoking and unattended, and looked around at the assembled cots, the beer cooler, the table of snacks and cake, and the now-silent tape player. At a gesture from him, several soldiers began to gather up the food and drinks. One reached down to pick up a beer and offered it to his commander. Obutu opened it, took a swig, and smiled approvingly.

"Take them!" he ordered.

A half dozen beefy and grim-faced soldiers seized the Peace Corps volunteers and roughly herded them into the waiting transport truck. Todd pulled away and protested, only to be slammed on the jaw by a rifle stock. Judy screamed.

Jeff shouted, "We are Americans! You can't do this! You'll hear from our government!"

"I shall count on it," Obutu said with a smirk.

Chapter 6

JAIL

From the journal of Eric Benton, November 4:

It's been two days since we were jailed in the detention center in the town of Lumbazo.

We don't know what happened to the young men from Tswana who were kidnapped by this General Obutu. I haven't seen them, but the scuttlebutt is that they were "drafted" into Obutu's military. How ironic—we all wanted to escape the draft!

They let me keep my journal, and so far they don't seem to care what I write in it.

I am in the same cell with Scott, Lex, Jeff, and Todd.

The girls are next door to us on the right. They don't segregate the women here, but we do seem to be the only whites. We have six cots, a john, a couple shelves, and little else. The food is not great, but edible. We are basically left here all day. They seem to want little from us. It's as if they are waiting for something to happen, and until then, they are just holding us here.

We spend a lot of time sitting around and talking, as we are now. We're getting to know each other pretty well. Heck, with one john and no shower, we're more familiar with each other than we ever wanted to be!

Scott and Jeff are lying on their bunks, Lex and Todd are sitting in one corner playing cards (they let us have cards after a day), and I'm in the other corner writing.

I like these guys a lot, for sure, but these close quarters are beginning to be a drag. We're dirty, and we're wearing the same clothes we were captured in, so you can imagine.

Next to us is a British reporter named Dennis Fletcher, who has been here more than a week. He doesn't know why he's been jailed, either, though he has some ideas.

We were scared at first, but now the biggest problem is the boredom. That and worrying about what's going to happen to us. We can't find out anything, but we keep thinking they must want us for something. At least two armed guards are always posted, one at either end of the corridor. They never talk to us or even react to us, and hardly look at us. We guess they don't speak English, so we can feel free to talk about most anything.

While Tarzan and the Waziri made their way to Opar, Eric Benton and the other Peace Corps volunteers found themselves in detention cells in Lumbazo, the capital and largest town in the territory. They were housed in a single-story cement block jail. Their section contained eight cells in a row along one wall of a five-foot-wide corridor. The cells faced a solid block wall, which apparently had another section of cells on the other side. At one end of their corridor stood a solid, battered iron door through which new prisoners, food, and any change in routine would be brought.

Each floor-to-ceiling cell door had vertical bars and a small horizontal slot through which food was passed. The two cell walls on their left and right consisted of cinder block and mortar, stained and filled with graffiti, rising to a height of about four feet from the floor, and the remaining space blocked with vertical bars running to the ceiling, so that they could see and talk to inmates in adjacent cells. It was how the Peace Corps volunteers were able to meet Dennis Fletcher.

The only other source of distraction to relieve the boredom was a small lone window in their rear wall, opposite the cell door. It was about six feet off the floor and looked onto the main street of Lumbazo, allowing the inmates to see very little but hear the noises of the bustling town—and freedom—outside.

They had not been there very long when the obvious questions began. "Scott," Lex asked, "are they gonna kill us?"

"Well, I think that if that's what they wanted to do, they would have done it by now."

"Then what are they gonna do with us?"

"I don't know."

Day after day, that question remained unanswered during the unvarying routine. No one visited them, and no one interrogated them during their empty days. The monotony was broken only by meals served twice a day by grim-faced guards who spoke no English and whose blank stares gave no hint of compassion or explanation.

Their only diversion was conversation. They wondered whether their government—or their families—knew where they were. They received no mail and were allowed to send none. In the adjoining cell, the older and more worldly-wise Fletcher availed them of what knowledge and insight he had in answering their questions.

"Who is this General Obutu?" was among the first questions the young Americans put to Fletcher after exchanging names and trading accounts of their capture.

"I don't know much about him," Fletcher told them. "He only started to get world-wide attention about two years ago, when he was named general of the army by Sefu Abadd, the fellow who ruled this province for several years. Then Abadd disappeared from the picture about six months ago. Nobody knows exactly why, though there are theories. Anyway, the next thing we know is that Obutu has declared himself ruler of the province. There have been stories of murders and beatings and extortion, but nothing confirmed. He keeps a tight wrap on news from the area."

"Our training didn't tell us much about Abadd, or a takeover by Obutu," said Scott.

"Well, that's not all that surprising, you know. Your American television doesn't exactly do a bang-up job covering world news, and when they do cover any of it, it's almost invariably been about Vietnam. Anyway, no journalist has been able to get near him, as far as I know, but most haven't wanted to because until now he's been a marginal figure. But if he's taken to incarcerating the likes of us, he's either a colossal fool or he's got some grand ambition. Either way, I wish I knew more."

"I still don't get why we're here," said Scott. "How are we a threat? We've just been jailed like common criminals."

"Not exactly. Haven't you noticed? Look around you. No Africans in this section."

"You mean the prison is segregated?"

"No. I mean our status is, well, special."

"How do you figure?" asked Jeff.

"Well, for one thing, they haven't beaten us, have they? Haven't you noticed the screams at night, muffled, as if they were coming from another building?"

"Sometimes, yeah," said Eric.

"I suspect there's another section where prisoners aren't treated so well. And we're fed better, I think."

"We are?" asked Todd.

"You've noticed that we often get fresh fruit? And the couscous or rice we're given doesn't seem to have any little critters in it. And the water seems clean. Let's just say that I've heard of worse conditions in other prisons. I think it's because we're European and American."

"So?"

"So we're a bargaining chip, I expect. They want to use us."

"For what?" Scott asked.

"Dunno. Possibly hold us for ransom, make demands, use us in negotiations for something else they want. I don't think they just randomly picked us out to toss in jail."

"Then why hasn't anything happened yet?" asked Scott. "Why are we still sitting here?"

"These things take time. Even if Obutu knows what he wants to do with us, and I'm not sure he does. He may still be trying to decide. From his point of view, there's no rush. People have been detained for months in prisons for no particular reason."

"Months…?" Lex said softly.

Fletcher added, "They haven't taken your pictures yet, have they?"

"No," said Scott.

"I expect they will, to prove you're all right. And when you are released, you won't be able to say you were badly treated."

"Does that mean we're safe? That we'll get out?" Lex asked nervously.

"Probably. But there's no telling. I'm pretty sure most tin-horn dictators don't want to cheese off the Americans by kidnapping their citizens, especially non-combatants."

"And what about reporters?" asked Eric.

"Well, I've heard of reporters in situations like this who have got released in a dog-and-pony show. And I've heard of some who have died in prison. I don't know."

Chapter 7

THE WART HOG

His Excellency General Obutu was no stranger to Tarzan of the Apes. Tarzan had heard the name before and had encountered the man a number of times over the years. As the ape man marched along the trail with the Waziri, he had a great deal of time alone with his thoughts, and his musings about Opar and the genesis of their quest led inevitably to the memory of the time he first encountered Obutu.

It was a long time ago. The ape man was visiting a favorite watering hole deep in the primeval jungle, an idyllic grotto that he often sought out for its tranquil beauty. That afternoon he was stretched out lazily in the soft grasses, leaning against a sun-warmed boulder, fading in and out of a refreshing nap. The towering limbs of the jungle giants that rimmed the edge of the glade provided cooling shade in the hottest part of the day. A few feet in front of him lay a spring-fed pond, its waters gently rippling and sparkling in the early afternoon light. The pond was rimmed with grassy shoreline and rocky outcroppings and knolls suitable for sunbathing or launching a dive. The water was deep enough for a swim, cool enough for a refreshing drink, clear enough to spear fish in.

Set upon the boulder next to him were his spear, his bow and quiver of arrows, and his woven grass rope, all of which he had fashioned with his own hands. Those items, plus his animal skin loin cloth and his father's hunting knife, sheathed at his waist, constituted the sum total of his worldly wealth. He wanted for nothing more. Indeed, Tarzan remembered that he

43

had been very content that day. Visits to this place were among the most pleasant and satisfying moments in his life. It was the kind of moment that he relished, and it made him long to keep returning to this primitive jungle, even after he had seen the civilized world and acquired the wealth to enjoy it.

He was roused from his pleasant torpor by a faint sound of commotion carried by the wind—animal squeals mixed with shouts. It did not sound like a hunting party, but it was so faint that he could not be certain what it was. He hoped that some expedition or safari would not come blundering into his little Eden.

Refreshed from his nap and sated from his morning hunt, the young ape man was in a mood to investigate. He rose, donned his weapons, leaped to one of a nearby tree's lower limbs, and swung himself up nimbly, like a gymnast, to another limb. From there, with the agility of the great apes among whom he was raised, he headed toward the sound through the middle terraces, that level of intertwining branches that were strong enough to support his weight yet high enough to conceal his presence and allow him to observe the ground below.

It was not long before he arrived at the source of the clamor. From his lofty perch, Tarzan looked down upon a half-dozen native boys, probably no more than twelve or thirteen years old, standing around a pit trap they had either dug or stumbled upon. The young ape man could not understand their words, but their situation was clear enough. They were displeased that a grizzled old wart hog had fallen into the pit, instead of some desirable trophy game. The harried creature ran back and forth along the few square feet in the bottom of the hole, leaping and scrabbling to scale the walls, but it could not. It squealed in anguish and frustration, and the more it squealed and leaped, the more the boys laughed at its plight. Though the pit was too deep for the animal to escape, it was shallow enough for the boys to reach it with their long hunting spears. They laughed and imitated its plaintive grunts as they repeatedly jabbed and stabbed at it, in its back, its haunches, its snout, even its eye. They drew blood again and again, and the hog squealed in pain.

One youth stood out in particular. He was broad and muscular, with a wide face, nose and cheekbones and a firm brow that produced an easy scowl. He was either in charge or had declared himself in charge, for he gave the orders. He was the one who cursed the hog most loudly for daring to fall into his trap, and he was the one who urged on all the others. Tarzan observed that when some of the youths hesitated to poke the hog, or wanted to stop, this one angrily pressed them to continue, laughing at the plight of the creature and shouting angrily at his fellows, sometimes through clenched teeth.

The ape man took an instant dislike to this sardonic youth, this punk (to use a word he would later learn in London). His manner was loud, boorish, and arrogant. Though Tarzan had not yet been exposed to the moral codes of polite civilization, he had already adopted an elementary ethos which held a reverence for life in all its beauty and diversity. Like all creatures, he would kill for food or defense, but wantonly slaughtering or senselessly tormenting a creature was repellent to him.

At length, the group abandoned its cruel amusement and walked off. As they receded into the jungle, Tarzan dropped from the trees near the pit and looked in on the wart hog. It lay on its side, slowly writhing in pain from many wounds, its blood darkening the earthen floor of the pit. With an arrow, he slew the pitiful creature to put it out of its misery. But he resolved not to let this incident end quite yet. The ape man was possessed of a certain impish humor, and he had often amused himself by playing tricks on tribesmen or other jungle travelers, particularly those whom he did not especially like. He took to the trees once again and swung off in the direction of the youths, who made no effort to conceal their whereabouts, loudly laughing, joking, and carousing on the trail.

Tarzan was often amazed by the lack of perception that even seasoned jungle dwellers exhibited. No matter how alert and observant expeditions or hunting parties might be while proceeding through the jungle, they rarely looked up. Thus the ape man could often travel with ease and skill through the middle terraces, scarcely twenty feet above their heads, undetected. Certainly these swaggering, obstreperous rowdies, confident of their own prowess, paid little heed to the thought that they might be stalked by a demi-god of the forest.

Tarzan followed them the rest of the day. He was curious to see where they had come from, but they were a long way from any village. Near dusk they proceeded to set up a camp for the night. They managed to crudely kill an eland and set a fire to roast it. Tarzan surmised that either they were vagrants with no tribe (unlikely at their age) or they had gone off from their village, probably without permission, to hunt and carry on.

Darkness fell, the embers of their fire faded, and their boisterous conversations diminished. As they arranged layers of grasses and bedded down for the night, Tarzan began to grow weary of watching them and had almost decided to move on when an opportunity presented itself. The cocky leader rose from his mat and proceeded to walk several yards off into the jungle to relieve himself. Tarzan seized the moment to swiftly move to a spot above him and then silently drop down behind him. In an instant, he cracked the youth across the jaw, stunning him long enough for the ape man to hoist him over his shoulder and carry him off.

Moments later, the remaining five sleeping youths were awakened by their comrade's anguished cries and pleas for help. Disconcerted, they stirred, looked around, and hastily roused themselves. It took several moments before they located the source of the screams. Many yards from their camp, they found him hanging upside down by his ankles twelve feet above the ground, suspended from a stout limb, cursing and shouting oaths at whoever had stuck him there, whoever failed to rescue him, and whoever else came to mind.

As the arrogant one writhed and screamed for rescue, the others on the ground debated how they would get him down.

Meanwhile, Tarzan of the Apes, watching the scene from the crook of a nearby limb, allowed a smile to break into a chuckle. He drank in the events for a few moments longer, until it became clear that the five on the ground would eventually figure out a way to climb up and free their friend, and then he vanished off into the jungle blackness, amused at the evening's entertainment.

Through most of the incident, Tarzan did not know the names of any of the youths. Only when he heard the others repeatedly call "Obutu!" when they saw him hanging in the tree did he realize that it was the name of the leader. He remembered the name. Whenever he recalled the event years later, Tarzan wondered whether he should have followed the rowdy group to its village. He came to wish that he had killed their cruel leader that day. At the time, however, the ape man's only regret was the loss of his grass rope. It would take him a long time to weave another, but it had been worth it.

Chapter 8

FLETCHER AND OBUTU

From the journal of Eric Benton, November 6:

Our cellmate, Dennis Fletcher the reporter, is fascinating. He's been to a lot of places and knows a lot. He tells us about the famous people he's met—including the Beatles!

He's probably as anxious about what's going to happen as the rest of us, but he takes it calmly, and his cool demeanor and good humor help to keep the rest of us calm and think that maybe things will be all right.

The only break in the routine came about the third day, when a lean African man in his twenties was brought in and put in the cell on the other side from Dennis. He keeps quiet and to himself. When Dennis tried to engage him in conversation, he shook his head and answered only in Yoruba. "Well, he's not European or American," Dennis commented. "So much for the segregation theory."

Keeping a diary?" Dennis Fletcher said as he peered through the bars and observed Eric writing.

"A journal, yeah," Eric replied.

"What do you write?"

"Oh, anything. Whatever I think of. I've certainly got enough time."

"Good habit," Fletcher said. "Keep it up. That's how writers get started."

"Really?"

"Sure. Writers keep notebooks and journals all the time. I've got about four or five nearly full ones in my satchel. Wish I had 'em now. Write everything—what you do, what you think, what you feel. Might come in handy. You never know."

Eric enjoyed talking to Fletcher, whose garrulousness helped considerably to pass the time.

"Why are you here in Africa?" Eric had asked him soon after they arrived.

"I came here to find Tarzan of the Apes."

"Who?" asked Lex, who overheard.

"You've never heard of Tarzan?"

"No. Who is he?"

"Well, believe it or not, that's a pretty complicated question. It depends on whom you ask."

"What do you mean?" asked Eric.

"Well, to some he is a legendary figure, something of a mythical hero. People tell incredible stories about him. Some say he can talk to apes. Some say he lives like a primitive wild man deep in the jungle. Yet I found him, in the person of one John Clayton, Lord Greystoke."

"So he's real. Not a legend?" asked Scott.

"Well, the man I met was an urbane English gentleman reserved in his manner and reluctant to talk about himself. I tracked him down to interview him and get him to tell the story, if there is a story to tell. But I guess that wasn't in the cards."

ON THE FIFTH DAY after the Peace Corps members arrived, a detail of three armed soldiers entered and stopped in front of Fletcher's cell. "Are you Fletcher?" asked one in broken, heavily African-accented English.

"Yes, Dennis Fletcher."

"You are reporter?"

"Yes. I've told you that."

"Your writing is published in magazine?"

"Yes. When my editor approves it."

"Do you wish to interview General Obutu?"

Fletcher let out a surprised smile. "Indeed I would, yes!" His eyes widened further when he saw that one of the guards carried his satchels, including his tape recorder and camera, which he handed over when the first guard unlocked the cell door.

"Come. His Excellency has granted you the privilege of an interview."

Fletcher exchanged a quick glance with the Peace Corps volunteers, then gathered his notebook and bags and accompanied the soldiers down the corridor and out the metal door. He was led out of the building, where they climbed into a waiting Jeep. They drove several blocks down the alternately dusty and paved streets of Lumbazo until they pulled up to what the guard called the "Presidential Palace." It was a massive stone and stucco four-story building that stood out in rather stark contrast to most of the wooden or brick buildings and ramshackle houses in the rest of the town. Flags flew from balconies that extended out from the third and fourth floors. A neatly mown lawn and landscaping of manicured trees and bushes fronted the building. Guards in crisp uniforms stood at attention at the entrance, flanking a canopy supported by brass poles.

Fletcher was escorted through the dramatic front entrance into the broad lobby and then to the left up a wide marble staircase with brass railings that curved grandly to the second floor overlooking the lobby. He was then led past several doorways opening into offices, to a wooden staircase. He could not help noticing that once he was past the grand foyer and staircase to the second floor, the décor slipped down a few notches, to worn carpet and walls of plaster and chipped paint. It was as if the building had been assembled in mismatched sections, the inner areas where the work was done being less important than the sections that could be seen from the outside.

As they ascended to the third and finally the fourth floor, Fletcher noticed that the décor and ambience once again improved, changing to newly-painted stucco walls, then to marble (or perhaps faux marble) and gilt edging. Guards in sharply pressed uniforms with berets were posted at the entrance to each floor. When they reached the fourth, the soldiers led him along a carpeted and wainscoted corridor to a set of tall double doors with two uniformed guards posted.

Fletcher was ushered into a room more like a meeting chamber or great hall than an office. It was massive, perhaps thirty feet across and fifty feet long. Suspended from ten-foot high ceilings were two glittering gold and glass chandeliers. The floor was wooden parquet, and the ceiling and walls were painted in a soft, creamy beige accented with gold trim. Along the walls, huge European landscape oils hung amid African artifacts such as weavings, decorative masks, and crossed spears.

At the far end, a tall pair of double doors opened onto a stone balcony facing the street below. Positioned on a Moroccan carpet near the center of the room, facing out to the balcony, was a large, ornately-carved mahogany desk with two large chairs facing it. Behind it stood General Obutu, resplendent in his clean, crisp uniform.

Obutu briefly flashed a broad grin and said, "Ah, Mr. Fletcher. Do come in. I've been expecting you. I trust your stay has been comfortable?"

"As a matter of fact, you've been keeping me in a prison cell," Fletcher said sardonically.

Obutu's grin faded a bit as he replied, "An unfortunate but necessary precaution, since we did not know what we might expect when you first joined us. We'll see what we can do about that." He waved Fletcher to sit in one of the two upholstered chairs facing the desk.

Fletcher immediately noticed a shiny, nickel-plated .45 caliber pistol lying prominently on the desktop. "Do you always keep a pistol on your desk?" he asked.

"Always. And two armed guards at the door, as you saw. A necessity in these volatile times, I'm afraid." Obutu produced a bottle of Glenfidditch and two crystal tumblers from the credenza against the wall behind him and asked, "Care for a drink?"

"Thank you. Don't mind if I do."

Obutu poured some into the two tumblers and passed one to Fletcher. "No one has told my story," he began. "I want my story told. It is a fascinating story, and you could get a Pulitzer for it. But I have one condition. You must allow me to see your finished manuscript before sending it on to your publisher. Do you agree?" Obutu's firm brow stared at the reporter.

Fletcher thought for a moment, and then agreed.

Obutu sat down, took a sip of his scotch, and continued, "My staff has done research to verify that you are whom you claim, and to learn of your work. I have decided to grant you an interview, so that you may educate the world about my glorious mission and the cause of African freedom and perhaps put to rest certain untrue rumors."

"Oh? And what would those be?" asked Fletcher, seizing upon the nugget Obutu had tossed him.

Obutu ignored the question and asked, "Why are you in Africa?"

"I came to interview Lord Greystoke."

Obutu paused for a moment. "Is he still alive? I've heard stories about him."

At this point Fletcher suspected that Obutu was adopting the same strategy he was, namely letting on less than he knew. It was part of the cagey cat-and-mouse game that interview subjects often played.

Seating himself, Fletcher set up his tape recorder, positioned his notebook and pencil, and said, "Well, shall we begin? Is Obutu your surname?"

"My name is Caesar Washington Obutu," the general replied, head up and chin slightly forward.

"And is that your birth name?"

"I have taken up the names of two generals, one a great emperor and the other the founder of a great democratic nation. Fitting, don't you think?"

"Weren't you a military official to Sefu Abadd, the ruler of this province, when he was elected?"

"I was his chief of staff and general to his army."

"Where is he? Suddenly, about six months ago, we read nothing about him any more, and no explanation of what happened to him."

"He...left the area. Ill health," the general replied, curtly.

"How did you happen to take over?"

"I have not 'taken over,' as you say. This is one of the great misconceptions Europe seems to have about me. The title was passed down to me. And in your article, you shall refer to me as President, not General. I shall be formally declaring my presidency in the near future."

"Then how is it that the title was...passed down? Why not hold an election?"

"You think like a European, Mr. Fletcher. For centuries, the tribal way in Africa has been for the chief to pass on his power either to his sons or to one he names, a trusted confederate. It is our custom."

"And it is important to do things the tribal way, as you say?"

"Africa has been subjugated by the white Europeans for too long. The African people must stand on their own, rule their own nations. Africa is the cradle of civilization, the place where mankind began. Why do Europeans think that they are so superior when they were living in caves and mud huts when Africans were building great cities and cultivating the land?"

"Well, Mr. President, I haven't been in your country long, but I've certainly seen a good deal of mud huts and poverty."

"That is because the people are victims of white capitalists and the vestiges of colonialism. The people must learn to stand on their own and develop their own economic base. They will be better off with self-rule."

"And you will bring this African self-rule to the people? Transform the country?"

"Not by myself. And not all at once, certainly. But bringing independence to this area, which we are calling for the moment the Congo Province, is a beginning. People will follow me and respect me. Under my rule, they will be free."

"That's very ambitious," Fletcher said noncommittally, taking a sip. "What have you been able to do so far?"

"I have begun to build an army—for defense, of course. And I have built roads. And schools. My next step is to consolidate the various tribes which are a holdover from the old days. I could do much more, but I need funds. It is expensive to run a country." Evidently, Fletcher thought, as he glanced at the palatial trappings in Obutu's office. "But I am currently expecting a large supplement to my coffers which will allow me to do much more."

"And where is this coming from?"

Obutu's gaze narrowed, and he said simply, "There are tribes who will pay tribute."

"So you feel you have popular support, then?"

His face broadened into a wide grin. "The people love me! They willingly give me their sons to serve in my army. I am the right one for the people of Africa! I can lead them into a peaceful, prosperous future!"

Fletcher looked up from his notepad. "Forgive me for stating the obvious, but a great many of them seem to be getting killed. For a revolution based on peace and love, there has certainly been a great deal of bloodshed."

Obutu threw back his head and let loose a hearty laugh. "You are such a hypocrite! Of course revolution is messy! Tell me that the history of Britain is not littered with bodies and bloodshed. Your greatest kings were all killers. Yet you would probably be the first to say your country is a shining example of a civilized nation. It is a nation founded on blood! Name me a nation that is not!"

"General, you seem to have built a great many prison cells—"

"Do not tax my good will with such trivial matters!" Obutu shot back, growing a bit vexed. "Every nation has prisons. Every society has criminals and misfits who must be controlled, for the sake of order and the greater good."

"But why have you imprisoned the American Peace Corps volunteers? They have done nothing."

Obutu's stern visage morphed into an unctuous smile. "Oh, that was something of an error. An overzealous lieutenant misunderstood my order to detain all outsiders. I am making arrangements for their release."

All he had to do, Fletcher thought, was to arrange for a key to be turned in a lock. But at the risk of irritating Obutu further, Fletcher let this explanation slide, though it contradicted every detail of the Americans' version, and moved on to more mundane questions for the moment.

Obutu granted Fletcher a full hour interview. All the while he sat with the general, the reporter wondered what he was going to do with the mass of prevarications, misdirection, and self-aggrandizement that the general shoveled at him. After he was returned to his cell, he worked most of the evening and all the next day, tapping away on his portable typewriter. Eric watched him often.

"Keepin' you awake?" Fletcher asked at one point.

"Nah. It's fine. At least somebody is getting something accomplished."

The guards allowed him to type uninterrupted, even fetching him additional paper.

On the second day, a tall, stately lieutenant in a medal-bedecked uniform appeared before his cell gate and said, "General Obutu has sent me to ask whether you have finished your article yet. He reminds you of the agreement that you would submit a copy to him."

Fletcher fished a sheaf of papers out of his satchel. "Ah, yes, here it is. You may give the general this copy." He passed it through the food slot.

The lieutenant took it and scanned the pages, reading phrases aloud in passable English:

> *President Caesar Washington Obutu is a man on a mission to save his people. As the ruler of the Congo Province following the departure of Sefu Abadd...*
>
> *...gracious, witty, and charming...*
>
> *...he described his struggle to raise the standard of living of his people, building roads and schools...*
>
> *...he spoke of the importance of self-rule and freedom...*

The lieutenant looked up from the manuscript and said, "This is very good. I am sure His Excellency will be pleased." He turned on his heel and strode out with the manuscript in hand.

"So glad you approve," Fletcher muttered, and then sat down to his typewriter and produced from his satchel a second folder of papers, inserted one into the carriage, and began to type.

Through the bars of his cell, Eric asked, "What are you writing now?"

Fletcher looked up from his notes briefly to smile wryly and say, "The real article."

Because of Fletcher's position at the table, nearly facing them, the Peace Corps volunteers could not see what he was typing. Nor were they curious, feeling that he would share it with them when he chose to. But another pair of eyes was intently curious about the words being typed on the portable Smith-Corona. The lean, taciturn African man in the cell adjacent to Fletcher's, who could see through his bars at what Fletcher was writing, tried to remain surreptitious as he watched the English phrases— which he understood full well—flow from Fletcher's fingers:

> *...arrogant dictator...*
>
> *...self-indulgent autocrat, given to mood swings...*

...after the sudden and mysterious disappearance of Sefu Abadd, rose to power in a legacy of violence and bloodshed...

...fancies himself the people's leader but lives in palace while his "people" suffer in poverty and ignorance...

THE NEXT DAY, the cell block was honored with a visit from the General himself. Obutu, accompanied by four armed guards, strode through the iron door and down the corridor to Fletcher's cell. He smiled broadly and said, "I am pleased with your article. Pack your things. You are free to go."

Fletcher stood up, a bit overtaken by surprise, but allowed a smile to break from his lips as he hastily pulled together his belongings. He looked at the Peace Corps students, smiled, and said, "I'll see what I can do to get you guys out of here." With a nod to Eric, he added, "Keep writing, kid." He walked out of the cell with Obutu's entourage.

Eric and the others rushed to the small windows in their cells and alternately stood on tiptoe to see what they could out in the street. The journalist and Obutu's detail emerged from the front of the detention building. Fletcher squinted a bit in the bright sunlight he was not used to. Obutu stopped and pointed to Fletcher's Range Rover, parked in the street several yards away.

"There you are," he said. "Washed and filled with petrol and ready to go."

At the sight of the general, many people in the street stopped what they were doing and stood, watching whatever spectacle might unfold. Fletcher, still a bit incredulous at his sudden release, looked about and tried to make eye contact with the young people squinting out of their tiny cell block window, but all they could see was his elated expression as he turned and began walking toward the waiting vehicle.

Fletcher was about a dozen yards away from them, his back toward them, when Obutu gave a small hand signal, where-upon the guard next to him raised his rifle and fired twice. The sharp echo of the rifle mingled with the gasps and cries of the onlookers. Fletcher was hit in the head and back. Cathie and Julie screamed as Fletcher fell to the dusty street, blood pooling around his pierced flesh.

The people in the street were shocked and agitated, some frozen in awe, some scrambling for safety.

Obutu took a half dozen steps forward toward the middle of the street. He turned slowly to the left and right to address all the onlookers, and said in stentorian tones, "This is the price you pay when you defame General Obutu! This man"—he gestured to the body of Fletcher—"would have spread lies and done dishonor to me and to you!" He turned to his lieutenant and said, "Let his body rot there for all to see!"

"Let his body rot there for all to see!"

Chapter 9

ON THE TRAIL

C louds sailed across the moon, and a cooling breeze wafting through the campsite stirred the smoky embers of the dying fire as Tarzan and the Waziri party rested on the fourth night of their journey. They had reached the highlands and had made their camp for the night on the highest ground so far, after partially ascending a hillside, thus affording them a striking view of the surrounding forested lowlands.

The recollection of his encounter with Obutu was only one among many thoughts and memories that swirled through the mind of the Lord of the Jungle on this expedition. Thinking of the ancient city also led Tarzan's mind to drift easily to La of Opar and, just as inevitably, to Jane Porter of Baltimore—the two remarkable women in his life.

La—the primitive barbarian high priestess, who spoke only her primitive language when he met her and only ever managed to learn halting English. Passionate, fiery, she was possessed of a voluptuous beauty and a sensuality that was elemental. Though he had not seen her in decades, her image in his mind was like a photograph: her skin, like his, bronzed and scarred from many encounters; her loins, like his, girded in animal skin pelts; her firm breasts covered at various times either by fur or hammered plates of gold or bronze; a jeweled dagger her weapon of choice.

And Jane Porter—elegant, refined, willowy, she of the stylish blonde hair and tailored clothing, educated in finishing school, possessed of wit and charm that endeared her to all who met her. She who was equally at home at a formal dinner party or a safari campfire, the one who had been able to bridge John Clayton's two worlds with an ease that La could never have managed.

It was this flexibility, this adaptability, which led John Clayton ultimately to choose life with her. Jane Porter was the one who allowed him to dwell in both of his worlds, the one who tolerated his regular forays into the jungle while she remained half a continent away in Europe or America on social visits or holidays.

He loved Jane with all his heart, yet expeditions like this inevitably stirred his dormant memories of La once again. Each of these beautiful women spoke to one of the dual sides of his person—the English lord and the demi-god of the forest. Each roused in him a passion and a yearning that could be instantly tapped in a moment of idle thought. It was only in moments like this that he felt a sense of time passing, and entertained however fleetingly the notion that perhaps he had lived too long.

Such were the thoughts of the Lord of the Jungle as he lay under the stars on a cool African night in that nebulous twilight between wakefulness and oblivion.

EARLY THE NEXT MORNING, as the tribesmen were arising and beginning breakfast, one of the sentries came rushing in with an expression of urgency on his face.

"Come! Look," he bade Tarzan and Dajan.

He led them to his post where, beyond a clump of trees, they could look down into the lowland they had traveled through the day before. From this position they could see miles of the jagged line of treetops in the forested expanses below.

"See it?" He pointed to a section of rugged forest about a half-day's journey behind their position. They observed a thin column of smoke rising toward the pale morning sky. "Somebody is out there, on our trail."

Tarzan climbed a nearby tree to gain a better vantage point and from that position regarded the smoke for a few more minutes before dropping down to join the others.

"Who could they be?" asked Dajan. "Are they following us?"

"We cannot be certain," replied the ape man. "They may be a safari or hunting party who happen to be in the area, unaware of us. If so, we can just let them alone and move on. Let us proceed another day. If they are still behind us tomorrow, then we will need to investigate."

The expedition journeyed another day through the dense jungle at their normal, though brisk, pace. Near dusk, they settled upon a spot to stop for the night and set up their camp. The camp was particularly quiet that night, alert for any unusual sounds that might denote intruders. The posted sentries were especially vigilant to note any sign of a party following them.

In the waning light, they noticed the same telltale campfire smoke in the distance, a half day's journey behind them. Someone was definitely following them. And there could only be one reason.

They next day the party split into two. Thirty of the Waziri men continued ahead toward Opar, bearing all their supplies. Tarzan, Dajan, and ten of the most experienced warriors, with a full complement of weapons, doubled back along the previous day's trail, heading in the direction of the smoke they had seen. They spread out over a wide arc and made their way in silence, moving with stealth bred of generations of hunting and tracking in the jungle, keeping to the concealment of tree trunk and leafy shrub.

It took longer than they expected to approach the party following them, who were not progressing nearly as fast as the Waziri. It became evident that this party's strategy was not to overtake the Waziri, but simply to keep behind them all the way to Opar, presumably allowing the Waziri to go through the effort of retrieving the gold and then ambushing them for it on the way back.

From time to time, Tarzan took to the trees to scout ahead, covering the distances more rapidly through the middle ter- races than men on the ground could, and reporting back to Dajan about what lay ahead.

Toward the end of the day, as he paused on a sturdy curved limb, he heard the noises of the advancing expedition. He noted their position and returned to report it to the Waziri, who were not far behind. He then took to the trees again to return and reconnoiter further. By that time, night had already begun to envelop the jungle, and it was too dark to see very far ahead, but he could tell from the smells and sounds that the expedition had halted and was setting up camp for the night, pounding tent stakes, starting a fire, and rattling cookware.

Tarzan desired a closer look, but the troop had pitched camp in something of a clearing, so that no branches strong enough to support him extended far enough over the encampment to allow him to hear what they were saying. He dropped lightly from the tree limb and moved nearer the camp, close enough so that he could hear. He peered through the cover of broad fronds at the scene illuminated by the central campfire, now blazing.

His suspicions were confirmed. It was a party of at least fifteen of Obutu's soldiers, quartered in military-style khaki bivouac tents. They had not yet retired for the night, but were gathered around the fire finishing their supper or walking to and from their tents. They chatted and joked as if they were on a pleasure outing, regaling each other about what they would do with their "share of the gold." Women. Cars. A huge feast.

"I know what I'd like to do!" one of them said.

"What?" asked another.

"Air condition the entire town!" They laughed.

Tarzan heard no more of their banter, because at that moment a sentry on his left appeared with leveled rifle and said, "Hey!"

As the ape man whirled to face the sentry, his momentary distraction prevented him from detecting a second sentry who sneaked up on him from his right and delivered a crack on the back of his head, sending him reeling to the ground.

Dazed, he looked up to see a soldier standing over him, saying, "Well, what have we here?" In the dim light, he was aware of two other soldiers, one on either side of him, pointing their rifles down at his head, the barrels barely an inch from each temple.

Tarzan's wrists were quickly bound behind him, his weapons were taken from him, and he was brought in to the camp, two rifle barrels trained on him at all times. The ape man berated himself for getting caught so easily. How could they have sneaked up on him? Had he not been alert and attuned to the sounds and movements around him? Were his jungle senses—the same ones that had kept him alive for so long and through so much—now diminishing?

He had, however, little time to reflect on such matters. He was escorted to the central campfire, where he was presented to the officer who was evidently in charge of the expedition, one Captain Batuuli.

"Who are you?" the captain asked.

"I know who he is," said one of the men holding a rifle to him, a sergeant. "He is Greystoke. He used to be called Tarzan."

"Why are you here?" Captain Batuuli continued.

"It was such a nice night, I thought I'd take a walk."

Batuuli raised his arm and delivered a backhand swat across Tarzan's face, snarling, "Do not mock me!"

"He is helping the Waziri. He's their honorary chief or something," the sergeant said.

"What are we going to do with him?" asked the other guard, a private.

"General Obutu will be pleased to see that we have him," the captain said.

"You want to bring him back?" said the sergeant. "That means we will have to feed him and watch him the entire way. It will be a lot easier if we kill him, and the general will still be grateful."

Tarzan said, "If you kill me, you will never get any gold."

"What?" asked Batuuli.

"I alone know how to reach the gold."

The captain stepped closer, looking into Tarzan's gray eyes, and said, "You lie. Someone else in the party must also know."

"And if you kill me," Tarzan continued, a cold calm in his voice, "the Waziri will be very angry with you."

"Sir, if he found us, the rest of the Waziri will too!" the sergeant said, a note of anxiety in his voice.

Captain Batuuli said with a smirk, still eyeing Tarzan, "Oh, we don't have to worry about them. We have guards."

At that instant a Waziri arrow sliced through the night air and pierced the captain's throat clear through to the other side. His mouth formed a silent gasp as he sank to the ground. In the next instant, before the sergeant could react, a Waziri war spear lodged in his back and he, too, fell. In reflex, he fired a shot into the air.

Tarzan quickly lifted a powerful leg and kicked the private backward into the burning logs of the campfire. Tarzan then turned to look down upon Captain Batuuli, who was writhing on the ground and gasping for his final breath, and said, "You were saying...?" before turning to dash off into the jungle to join his rescuers.

A volley of Waziri spears and arrows was unleashed from the darkness. The camp erupted in chaos. Guards were cut down in an instant. Soldiers shouted and dashed about in a frenzied effort to rally against an attack that came from they knew not where. Everywhere, it seemed.

Tarzan plunged into the darkness of the jungle bordering the camp, where he was met by Waziri comrades who swiftly cut his wrists free.

As soldiers rushed to or from their tents and scrambled to seize their weapons, amid shouts and curses and hastily-framed orders, Waziri tribesmen picked out individual targets smoothly, efficiently, their aim honed from years of having only one try at bringing down a quarry.

A few soldiers managed to seize their weapons and tried to fire, but the Waziri were concealed by the night and their ebony skin, so that the four or five shots discharged were in vain.

Death sailed through the night air. Soldier after soldier fell to the Waziri missiles. A few soldiers managed to locate some of the Waziri tribesmen in the bush and engaged them in brief hand-to-hand combat. Tarzan, freed from his bonds, wrested one soldier off the back of a Waziri and threw him headlong into a tree. He seized another who was raising a pistol to a tribesman and wrenched the pistol arm back until it snapped, allowing the tribesman to finish him off.

It was over in a few minutes. The camp that had been a flurry of activity and oaths and panic and cries of agony now lay in grim silence. Upchurned dust and smoke from the fire rose slowly to the upper boughs and beyond into the jungle night. The conquering Waziri tribesmen emerged from their places of concealment and advanced into the camp, lighting some of their torches from the fire to better illuminate the scene.

They slowly walked among the bodies strewn around the campground, assessing the damage. "All dead," Dajan said, grimly.

"You came just in time," Tarzan said. "I regret getting caught."

"We watch out for each other," Dajan replied with a smile, and then asked, "Should we collect the weapons?"

"No," said Tarzan. "If any of them are ever found in your possession, Obutu will know what happened. Leave everything as it is. The hyenas will find them."

All the Waziri tribesmen in the party survived the attack, though some had been wounded. Nevertheless, as Dajan watched his men retrieve their spears and arrows from the lifeless bodies, he stared somberly at the carnage.

"What else would have happened?" Tarzan said, seeing his friend's grim visage. "They would have followed us to the gold, and then what? No doubt they intended to ambush us. At least this way they will be presumed lost in the jungle, and no one can say otherwise."

No one in the party, however, could know that the jungle lord's assessment was incorrect.

It happened that three soldiers coming back from patrol on the far side of the camp from the Waziri's main approach had been busily engaged in conversation and smokes when the battle erupted. Hearing the ruckus, they dashed closer to the camp and looked aghast at the scene. Having grown up hearing tales of the Waziri's reputation as fierce warriors, they gave not the slightest thought to aiding their comrades. Instead, fearful for their lives, they turned tail and bolted into the dark jungle undetected.

But not before one of them managed to grab the expedition's radio.

Chapter 10

OPAR

The night after the skirmish with Obutu's men, they all sat around their campfire for some time discussing the events of the day and the likely events to come. Several of the younger Waziri who had not been to Opar asked many questions about what the city was like and what had happened there over the years.

One inquisitive young warrior asked, "Tarzan, you say that the city has been rocked by earthquakes and that it has been many years since you were there."

"Yes," replied the ape man.

"What if another earthquake has occurred and the entrances to the treasure chambers are all blocked? If we cannot reach the gold, then what do we do?"

"He makes a good point," said Dajan.

"I have been thinking about that very possibility," replied the ape man, "and I think I have an idea. Regrettably, it will add days to our journey."

Tarzan explained his plan. After many questions and considerable discussion, they reached their consensus. Yes, they agreed with the ape man.

The plan required them to divert from their route and travel two days to the south, to the river port town of Pattersonville. There Tarzan sought out a merchant with whom he had dealt in the past and with whom the credit of Lord Greystoke was good. The expedition was outfitted with dynamite, blasting caps, fuses, black powder, picks, shovels, and lengths of rope.

The tribesmen packed these supplies in their hammock-like slings and bore them back out through the jungle to resume their trek to Opar.

The journey to Opar took them across many miles of jungle and plain. They climbed craggy hills and made their way along narrow paths that wound around cliff faces and steep escarpments. At length, after two more weeks of hiking, they reached the last and most challenging natural barrier, a narrow gorge that cut between two rock cliffs towering hundreds of feet above them. The V-shaped pass was barely wide enough for a man to pass through, and was strewn with rock, so that they were compelled to strap onto their feet the leather coverings their women had made for the purpose. They squeezed through the channel and emerged on the other side near dusk, facing the narrow, bleak valley, the so-called "forbidden valley," filled with clusters of scrub trees and rock, across which lay their destination. They rested in preparation for the last leg of their journey and rose very early, well before dawn, to make the trek during the coolest part of the day.

They set out across the expanse when it was still dark, the moonlight barely illuminating the way, so that they needed to employ torches. Tired but undaunted, and eager at the prospect of reaching their goal, they pressed on across the miles of rocky, boulder-strewn flatlands, until the glint of dawn began to highlight their goal in the distance—the walls and towers of the lost and mysterious city of Opar.

For a moment, shrouded in mist, the city appeared vaguely as it once must have to those who saw it in its prime—a mysterious, almost mystical, walled temple rising from the floor of the desolate landscape, with spires and towers suggesting a magnificence that might be the dwelling place of gods. But as the expedition approached and the climbing sun burned off the morning haze and illuminated the walls and towers in sharper relief, it became clear that the ancient, empty city was even more of a ruin than it had been the last time the ape man and the Waziri had visited it, years ago. The outer walls had half crumbled into rubble that lay mounded in piles at their base. The portions of walls that still stood were overgrown with vines that had eaten away at the mortar, loosening it in many places so that the walls were riddled with cracks, and sizeable sections had come loose.

Opar presented no grand entrance gate. The party approached the city and sought out the narrow, well-concealed entrance through the decaying wall. Emerging into a courtyard, they walked down dusty, rubble-strewn streets, some of them still inlaid with gold.

It was also evident that at some time since they last visited, an earthquake had hit the city again, at least as strong as the one which had imperiled Tarzan many years before. One entire section of the east portion of buildings had been rent asunder. Several great rifts had opened up in some of the walls, and sections of some structures had been stove in or crushed from falling debris.

They approached cautiously, weapons poised, advancing carefully through the streets, surveying left and right as they walked. The younger Waziri, their heads having been filled by the elders with tales of beast-like men and human sacrifices, were apprehensive and wary, their hearts palpitating. But though they scanned every shadow and escarpment, no such threat emerged.

"It's really deserted," said one.

"I'm glad," allowed another.

As they had suspected—indeed, hoped—no one had been there. The party found no sign at all of any occupant, any intruder, any predator having disturbed the accumulated dust and grit. The entire city had the stillness of a crypt. The visitors had never heard such silence in the midst of the jungle wilderness.

Fortunately for the expedition, enough of the city was still standing that the side streets and lower chambers seemed accessible. The dynamite would evidently not be needed. The deteriorated condition of Opar, however, had confirmed the ape man's fears that if the last quake had not toppled all the walls and sealed up the lower chambers, the next one might. Accordingly, they planned to remove as much of the gold as practicable to a location outside the city.

Tarzan led the Waziri through a courtyard and down narrow side streets into the temple. They stopped to peruse the massive stone altar about which the younger Waziri had heard so many tales. They continued down a series of stairways hewn out of solid rock. Their eyes needed some moments to adjust to the darkness, having spent the day under the African sun. The air turned refreshingly cool rather quickly, the dampness increasing as they descended.

Their torches barely lit the Stygian darkness. Once again, the younger Waziri who had never been there were anxious as they brushed along the lichen-encrusted walls and squinted around the corners. Even in the smallest homes in Kumali, they had never been quite so enclosed. Some were fearful of the long, dank, cramped passageways, but the older tribesmen assured them that, yes, all this effort would be worthwhile.

Mostly in single file, they passed dungeons whose cells had long ago held prisoners or beasts. The farther in they ventured, the more foul and musty the air became. Their feet stumbled upon dusty bones. Several times, when they directed their torches to the side, they could see skull fragments and disjointed bones half-buried in the dust.

As the procession turned a corner, the warrior Matu, near the front, hesitated for an instant at something the ones behind him could not see. Then he jerked back and exclaimed, "Aaah! He's still alive!"

The half dozen younger Waziri behind him froze in their tracks, the panic in their eyes visible even in the dim torchlight. The older Waziri men looked at them. Tarzan and Dajan began to laugh, and then so did the other veterans.

"Don't worry," Matu said, laughing heartily. "There's nothing alive down here!" They resumed their trek past more cells, all quite empty.

At last they reached the first of the treasure troves, a narrow, musty chamber piled nearly half-full of blackened, roughly-cast ingots whose color matched the grime on the floor and walls. A few torches held in the doorway faintly illuminated the darkness, and the stacked bars might have been slag for all that they glittered. One Waziri took out his knife and scraped off the layers of dust and grime on one bar to reveal streaks of yellow that glinted in the torchlight. They looked at each other and grinned. It was still here.

They located more chambers that contained hundreds of ingots, all having been cast and stacked by long-dead hands. From all indications, some might not have seen the light of day for centuries. The men formed a brigade to pass bar after bar out from its crypt along the corridors and out into the light of day and, ultimately, outside the city walls. They allotted an entire day to this endeavor, which was all they could lest they not return by Obutu's deadline.

The Waziri were extraordinary and energetic laborers with considerable stamina. They chanted songs to cadences pounded out by their drummer. Despite the heat, the sweat, and the demanding physical labor their massive task required, their spirits were high. Tarzan of the Apes worked along with them, his strength clearly undiminished and his stamina as hale as that of the youngest Waziri.

They amused themselves with the realization that, clearly, Obutu did not grasp the vastness of the treasure of Opar. Each bar weighed about twelve pounds, and at current market prices, the forty tribesmen plus Tarzan would be carrying home an amount equivalent to at least three times what Obutu had demanded. But they were not about to enlighten him on that score.

They carried the precious ingots more than a mile west of the city, near the edge of the jungle that encroached upon the barren wasteland. There, after setting aside the amount they would take back, they buried all the remaining gold of Opar. With the skills gleaned from centuries of jungle life, they concealed their tracks and constructed various natural markers which would be recognizable to fellow Waziri who might later return to the site, but which would not be given the slightest notice by a casual observer passing by who did not know upon what ground he trod. Then the expedition set up camp for the night and posted a guard on the gold.

After such a monumental task, the tribesmen would have preferred a sizeable celebration, but their priority was to get as much rest as they could that night. Moreover, they had only the provisions they carried in with them, since they would have to venture a day or more into the jungle before they could expect to bag fresh meat. Any festivities would have to be deferred until a more suitable time.

They rose with the dawn and did not bother lighting a fire, since their breakfast consisted of the last of the jerky and bread they had. They packed up their weapons and their hammocks with supplies, including their tools and the remaining unused sticks of dynamite. Each man packed two gold ingots into a harness specially fashioned for the purpose out of tanned hide and slung it on his back. It was decided that they would primarily carry smaller ingots weighing twelve to fourteen pounds each, rather than the larger forty-pound ingots, because they would be less strenuous to carry on the journey back that would be arduous enough without their burden.

As they all stood ready to move out, Tarzan of the Apes took one last look at the city which held such powerful memories for him—the city where he had met La, the city where both he and Jane Porter had nearly lost their lives, the city whose wealth had sustained generations of Waziri beyond the wildest imaginings of its builders.

He turned silently to face the way ahead and joined his Waziri comrades as they set out, again in a double line, across the surrounding barren flatland. It was not long before they launched into tribal chants to quicken their pace through the desolate wastes, until they reached the deeper forest and the hills and valleys beyond.

Chapter 11

SLAVERS

The visit to Opar and the thoughts of Jane that the journey stirred reminded Tarzan of the other time in the past that he had encountered Obutu.

It was years after the incident with the wart hog. Tarzan and Jane had married and established their intercontinental relationship. He resided with her in London for a few months each year when he attended to Parliament business and Clayton family matters, though he returned to Africa as often as he could. She remained in London, or visited her family in America, or joined him at his African estate because she, too, had found much to love in the Dark Continent.

It was during one of his London stays with Jane that they attended a dinner party given by a business associate of the Porter family. Unfortunately, it was also attended by distant, rather boorish relatives of Lord and Lady Greystoke. During the course of the evening, the host pressed Clayton about what his "African business" consisted of, a subject about which the lord had always been purposely vague. Feeling the effects of a particularly good burgundy, the Greystoke relative also proceeded to hold forth with his opinions about Africa in general and the African people in particular, peppering his remarks with references to "ignorant savages" and "godless primitives." It was something of a source of embarrassment that his relatives could not refrain from chiming in with such phrases as "those people" in a pejorative way.

Clayton grew irritated with the conversation and with the supercilious air that his host and kinsman took on. He believed that he had held his tongue appropriately, but Jane felt that in his looks and his manner he had been less than entirely polite. At any rate, they had a bit of a row about it afterward. Though it did not cause a rift in their relationship, the result was that Clayton resolved to leave for Africa rather earlier than usual that year, feeling as he always did that life in the primitive jungle, even with its tribulations and challenges, was infinitely more satisfying than navigating the courses of polite society.

Less than two weeks later he found himself deep in the interior of the Dark Continent, sitting around the bonfire in the Waziri village, feasting and drinking the native beer with his old friend chief M'Bala and the tribal elders, his belly full of antelope and wildebeest.

"There have been better times," the usually ebullient M'Bala was compelled to report when the conversation got around to recent events. "My son was killed by a leopard. I have no heir now."

"You will have to pick a successor," Tarzan said, and then added, with a chuckle, "or see about siring another son!"

"You missed Dajan's wedding," M'Bala went on. "Kerah is a fine bride."

"I will see them before I leave," replied Tarzan. Looking around at collapsed huts and downed sections of the great encircling wall, he added, "I see you've suffered some damage."

"The rainy season has been unusually heavy. You just missed a great storm. As you can see, we have much damage to repair."

"I can help you with that," Tarzan offered, taking a sip of his beer.

M'Bala added, "There is also another concern."

"Oh?"

"We have received reports of a few villages being raided up north. People being taken away. I do not know what to make of this news."

"Why?"

The chief's countenance grew grimmer. "It may mean nothing. But if someone is rounding up villagers and carrying them off, it may be slavers. It could pose a grave threat to the tribe. If they were closer I would send a party to investigate, but right now we are busy with the storm damage, and many crops are ready to harvest. I cannot spare men."

Tarzan said, "I could go."

"I would not ask you to do that."

Tarzan smiled. "You have not asked. I will do it as a favor. Alone, I can move quickly and reconnoiter unseen. As you say, it may pose a threat to the tribe."

M'Bala smiled broadly and replied, "Once again, the Waziri tribe is indebted to you, my friend!"

Tarzan left early the next morning, the Waziri having stocked his quiver full of arrows and provided him with a newly woven coil of rope and spare bowstring.

The ape man coursed swiftly through the jungle terraces for days, stopping only when necessary to kill game or rest. He visited several villages en route and learned that there had indeed been raids on villages and reports of people taken away in bondage, possibly to work in mines or be sold as slaves.

He also took the time to re-establish his relationship with a tribe of great apes through whose territory he passed, an offshoot of the tribe that had raised him and with whom he could communicate elementary questions such as whether anyone had passed through and how many.

On the third day, Tarzan located a village that had been raided and learned from its people that a group of African men with rifles and other firearms and wearing western clothing had attacked the village and taken about two dozen men and women northward. Tarzan headed off in the direction the villagers indicated, and it was not long before he found the trail of the party. He followed it until he came upon them. He encountered a bound and huddled troupe of villagers shuffling along the trail, herded by perhaps seven or eight burly Africans cursing them and prodding them with rifles. Tarzan remained in the middle terraces of the overarching trees, high enough to observe undetected, and followed them.

The party stopped at the valley of a small river, a rather distinctive area with large, jutting boulders and a grassy sward. Tarzan suspected that this was a rendezvous point and was proved correct when about an hour later another party of men approached from the west.

This party was a truly motley group, an ill-assorted collection of rogues and ruffians. Their leader and several of his lieutenants were clearly Arab, wearing robes and keffiyehs. Two even carried curved scimitars in their gun belts. Yet the eight or nine others were Asian and European, addressing each other in an array of tongues including English, Spanish, Japanese, several African dialects, and some language Tarzan could not recognize. Some wore safari clothing, and some were dressed in mismatched pieces of various uniforms, ragged and worn, possibly stolen. All were coarse in their manner and rugged and grizzled in their appearance, having evidently spent a long time in the wilderness. Tarzan had seen their types before. They may have been mercenaries, or treasure hunters, or poachers, but they never meant anything good.

A tall, swarthy Arab with a gray-flecked beard approached the prisoners and their captors. One of the African raiders stepped forward to greet him. It took Tarzan a moment, but it dawned on him that the stolid, beefy man who greeted the Arab was the same reckless youth who years before had tormented the wart hog—Obutu.

So now he is trading in human lives, thought the ape man.

They exchanged words which Tarzan could not hear. The Arab leader, who was referred to as Ahmad, waved his hand, and a lieutenant produced a small, decorative box with an ornate, hinged lid. Ahmad presented it rather ceremoniously to Obutu, who opened it. Inside was an assortment of gold coins, jewels, and what appeared to be European currency. It looked like quite a tidy sum. Tarzan wondered what the going rate for human flesh was. Obutu smiled and muttered some appreciation.

Ahmad's men and Obutu's men commenced to pitch their tents and set up a common camp for the night on the spot. They had evidently chosen this site as their rendezvous point because of its suitability for such a purpose. The slavers' Bedouin-like tents were set up on one side of the sward and the African raiders' more military, bivouac-like tents on the opposite. They built cooking fires, and soon the aromas of cooked meat and spicy stews wafted through the jungle night. Later, bottles of liquor were passed around, and the raiders and their new partners shared laughter and coarse camaraderie as they reveled in the profits that they had made or expected to make.

The Arab leader and Obutu shared a bottle and became fast friends. Their common language was English, and from various vantage points Tarzan was able to learn many details about their operation as the evening wore on. His suspicions were confirmed. The Arab-led misfits were indeed slavers, rounding up blacks to be sold to wealthy sheiks and entrepreneurs in Morocco or Egypt or Saudi Arabia, or whoever else could afford such indulgences. Obutu was eager to endear himself to his new-found benefactor and generously offered to reveal the locations of villages particularly vulnerable to conquest or to describe places where people gathered and would be caught off guard, making them easy pickings.

As they laughed and talked into the night, Tarzan of the Apes observed and pondered all of this from his lofty perch. He felt nothing but contempt for these marauders, this plague upon the jungle. The idea of human trafficking was abhorrent to him, and he knew that if these raiders were allowed to continue, more and more innocent lives would be threatened. But how could he stop them alone? He would wait for an opportunity.

At length Obutu retired, and the Arab Ahmad rose from the fire, turning to stagger away, humming. But he did not head for his tent. He teetered toward the area where the captured villagers were kept, crouched and bound together. He moved unsteadily along the row of forlorn men and women, stopping when he caught sight of one young woman, perhaps nineteen or twenty. When he gazed upon her, she averted her eyes.

"Look at me," he ordered. She turned her head upward to reveal large, dark eyes and smooth, comely ebony features. Her lip trembled.

The Arab ordered two of his lieutenants guarding the prisoners to seize the girl and pull her out away from the group and drag her toward his tent. He commanded them to set her down upon some soft grasses just far enough away from the fire so that he could still see her face in the light. He stood over her, eyeing her up and down, and said, "Hold her down." He unbuckled his gun belt, dropped it, and began to undo his robe. The girl, restrained by a soldier on either side, gasped and began to cry, "No! No!"

"Quiet!" the Arab snarled, "or I will cut your tongue out. You will need to get used to this. It is your fate." Ahmad had removed his robe and was just about to remove the loose shirt underneath. He leered at the girl, chortling. "Besides, you will enjoy this."

Suddenly the expression on Ahmad's face shifted from a lascivious grin to a pained grimace. At the same instant, the girl's countenance transformed from squinting revulsion to wide-eyed horror.

A long, straight arrow had hissed through the night and lodged itself in the black heart of the Arab slaver. He clutched at his breast. His shirt darkened with a crimson stain, and he fell upon the ground.

The girl screamed.

"We're under attack!" someone yelled. Cries and shouts of confusion and panic followed for several minutes. Every mercenary slaver, every henchman of Obutu, sprang up and seized his weapon, looking around, poised to retaliate. They looked up into the trees but saw nothing but the dappled moonlight, heard nothing but the night breeze rustling the leaves. As silent minutes passed, it became evident that the solitary missile, launched from they knew not where, constituted the lone assault.

In order to conceal his own anxiety, Obutu barked at a few of his younger men to stand guard before he went into his tent.

The camp slept restlessly that night, the kidnappers all keeping their weapons close at hand.

The Lord of the Jungle had wished only to reconnoiter and not reveal his presence, but he had felt compelled to save the girl. Now that his hand was forced, he felt no compunction about having brought down the chief slaver. That kind of man was a scourge on the jungle, he thought, and now it occurred to him that if he played his cards right, the consequences of this sudden move might be used to his advantage.

THE PARTY RESTED UNEASILY THAT NIGHT. They started out early the next morning, their conversation filled with talk of the end of their trek and the profits of their labors they would enjoy, though whether that choice of topic was genuinely foremost in their minds or whether it was an effort to mask their anxiety over the mysterious slaying of Ahmad, no one could say.

They forged ahead along the trail, several mercenaries in the lead, several of Obutu's men in the rear, and the remainder on either side, with the bound prisoners hobbling along in the center. They had proceeded only an hour or two when again, as suddenly and mysteriously as the night before, a single arrow whizzed in and struck one of Obutu's men in the back, penetrating deeply. As he sank to the ground, several women captives gasped or shrieked. The mercenaries and Obutu's men, more angry than shocked, raised their weapons and fired volleys into the surrounding jungle. They pumped lead until the air above them was a blue haze and the jungle echoed with the report of their rifle cracks. But they saw no result. The party took cover and for several minutes scanned the enveloping foliage, seeing and hearing nothing. Once again, no further attack.

"It's the forest demon!" one of the blacks said.

Some of the Africans with Obutu began to murmur about this demon, a spirit of the forest whom they had evidently offended and who they now feared was going to kill them all. Obutu tried his best to quell such rantings, lest his mercenary allies think ill of him. He, too had heard such tales of a forest devil but had—until now—given them no credence.

They paused at midday for rest and food near a cluster of fallen jungle giants and broad-leafed ferns and palms on gently rising and falling terrain. The group spread out in small knots to chat. One of the Arabs walked off a bit into the forest to relieve himself. Ahmad's lieutenant who had taken charge of the expedition, one Fayid, ordered the group to move on when one of the mercenaries said, "Where's Muhammad?"

They called to Muhammad, the missing man, but received no answer. They fanned out to look for him for several minutes, calling his name, to no avail. At length, Fayid, who was eager to get out of the jungle and enjoy the rewards ahead, ordered the party to move on. "We cannot look for him forever," he said. "If he is stupid enough to wander off, let him find his own way back. More of the share for us."

They continued to walk along, shouting "Muhammad!" at intervals and listening for replies that never came. The raiders expected to find him, too, with an arrow in his back. But since they had not seen him at all, some of them began to console themselves with the explanation that he had been attacked by a big cat or other predator. But, murmured others, how is it that we heard no sounds of such an attack?

They trudged on for a mile or two in a heightened state of apprehension. A few of the more superstitious prisoners began to moan that their captors had offended the god of the forest and they were all going to perish. "Shut up," said Obutu, "or you will be the next to die!"

Suddenly something dropped from above, plummeting down and landing with a thud on the trail a few yards ahead of them. The mercenaries at the head of the party, though tempered by the wild as they were, let out a gasp when they saw it. Two of the women prisoners screamed.

Lying on the jungle floor was the body of Muhammad, his neck broken, his eyes staring vacantly upward.

Tarzan of the Apes, in the trees above, saw the shock pass through the party, as he had expected, and the ghost of a smile played upon his lips.

THEY STOPPED TO MAKE CAMP for the night, having arrived at the spot where they would part company in the morning. Obutu and his men would return west to their homes, and the mercenaries and their captives would continue north. Once again, the mongrel company of mercenaries and Obutu's African raiders set up their respective tents and cook fires. As the evening wore on, their earlier fears of the "forest demon" began to ebb, chiefly a result of the liquor being passed around, even as the demon prepared to make another mysterious visit.

Tarzan crept stealthily from the darkness of the jungle to the edge of the camp and approached one of the tents, the one farthest from the campfire. Earlier he had seen one of the slavers, a big Swede reeling with drink, trundle clumsily toward this tent. In the darkness just outside the rear of the tent, Tarzan paused to listen. He could hear the heavy, regular breathing of a man inside, deep in sleep. He saw no one else around, all the rest of the kidnappers still carousing at the fires and the captives bound and huddled on the other side of the encampment.

Leaving his rope, quiver, and bow nearby, Tarzan untied one of the tent support ropes, lifted the bottom of the canvas tent wall, and slipped inside. He needed to creep silently only a few steps until he reached the prostrate figure. Drawing his knife, he slit the throat of the sleeping kidnapper and then melted away into the jungle night as stealthily as he had arrived.

About an hour later, as the fires were waning and the last of the camp was retiring, the Swede's tentmate staggered into his tent and beheld the bloody corpse on his sleeping mat. His horrified cries instantly alerted the entire party. Several raiders emerged from their tents in their underwear, groggy from sleep and drink, hastily seizing their rifles. In the span of a few moments, the raiders all had a look at their comrade slain right in their very midst, and their fears grew.

From somewhere up in the trees, a loud, resonant voice boomed, "Release the prisoners or you will die!"

"Who is that?" several said. They looked up and around, some merely curious, but many apprehensive.

A moment later, from an entirely different position, they heard the voice boom the same message, but in an African dialect that Obutu and his men knew full well. Then from another direction, the warning came again, in French.

The raiders crouched and cautiously looked around, grasping their weapons tightly. "How many of them are there?" they muttered. "Where are they?"

"Show yourself!" Fayid called in English, his head tilted upward. "We do not fear your empty threats!" He paused for a moment, and hearing nothing, added, "Come out and we will talk! I do not bargain with voices in the dark!"

"There is no bargaining," the voice resounded from the arboreal heights. "Release the prisoners now, or die!"

Fayid responded by firing a round in the general direction of the voice.

What happened next is the stuff of jungle legend, having been told and retold and embellished around campfires for years, so that over time even those who witnessed the event were unsure of what transpired. Some say the forest demon opened his mouth and there issued from it a piercing, guttural cry so frightful that it summoned demons from the underworld. Some insist a lion or other great jungle animal roared and frightened apes into stampeding.

Most accounts agreed that great hairy beasts came charging in from the jungle to wreak havoc on the camp. Some said it was a single great ape, but most were convinced it was more, perhaps as many as five or six. Whatever it was, it moved so fast in the half-darkness that no one got a close look, or wanted one.

In a fury of growling and gnashing, the bestial force thrashed the camp, overturning tents and knocking men aside like so many straw dummies. Guns were fired, but that did not deter the onslaught.

The suddenness and fierceness of the attack sent the jungle-hardened mercenaries into a frenzied panic. The night was instantly filled with ferocious growls and shouts and cries of men in pain.

At the same moment, a tall, nearly naked bronzed figure with a shock of black hair dropped from the trees into their midst and became a whirling frenzy, lashing out furiously at slavers distracted by the assault. In a barrage of flying arms and powerful kicks, he dispatched raiders one by one, cracking limbs and smashing heads against trees. Three of Fayid's men immediately fell to his snarling fury. Another mercenary came rushing toward him, but the figure's slashing blade made short work of that attacker, too. He then whirled to slice the ropes that bound the captives, so that they, too, could rise up against their abductors, making short work of any of them who had not already been dispatched by the white stranger or a marauding beast.

In the fray, the flaps from one of the downed tents landed in the fire and ignited. The tent flared up, and the fire spread to other tents, so that much of the turmoil was illuminated in flames and dramatic shadows.

Obutu beheld the decimation that was taking place before his eyes and did not hesitate to make his choice. In the confusion, he and two henchmen scurried off into the jungle.

The bestial force disappeared just as quickly and mysteriously as it had arrived, leaving only scattered and smoldering camp debris. Tarzan looked around at the damage, and from all appearances the slavers and their minions were all dead or run off, their hopes as dashed as their bodies on the ground. Tarzan did not bother to count or examine the bodies, and only years later realized that Obutu had survived. He felt no need to linger, for the slave ring had been broken up and there was the business of returning the newly freed people to their homes.

Tarzan of the Apes had learned something about Obutu from this encounter, however. He knew that this Obutu cared nothing for the African people and had only his own interests at heart.

And as for Obutu, he did not know who this naked white man was, though it would not be long before he would hear tales of his exploits. But he never bought into the lore of a white demi-god of the forest. To him, this ape man was just an interloper who had foiled his plans for riches. He did not know where to look to find this white lord, but he was certain of one thing—if he ever crossed paths with this meddler again, he would kill him.

Chapter 12

DURESS

From the journal of Eric Benton, November 25:

We've been locked up here for over three weeks now, and it's really starting to suck.

We still don't know what they're going to do with us.

I used to say I was glad to get to know these Peace Corps workers, but I have to say now that I think we're getting to know each other a little too well.

We're tired, we're dirty, we're hungry, we're lonesome. And we're scared.

The five Peace Corps men sat huddled on the floor of their jail cell or stretched on cots, wearied and bored. In the cell next to them, the two women also sat, equally wearied and bored. They had all been wearing the same jeans or shorts with T-shirts or tank tops and denim jackets for more than three weeks, and the sweat from the humidity and poor ventilation in the detention facility made the entire space dank.

Todd Fitzgerald, the engineering student who now looked more like a vagabond in his scruffy clothing and month-old beard, said to no one in particular, "I wonder how our little village is doing. They were just starting to trust and like us."

"Yeah, I wonder what happened to them," said Scott Gordon, the AD and oldest of the group. "I hope your well is still working."

Eric said, "I wonder what happened to our stuff?"

Hunched in the corner shuffling a deck of cards, Scott asked Lex Cooper, sitting opposite him, "Want to play another game?"

His face in a scowl, Lex said, "Ah, I'm sick of playing cards. And I'm sick of this place. When are we gonna get out of here?"

"We don't know," said Scott. "Just feel lucky to still be alive."

Lex groused, "If I hadn't come over from my village for the party, I never would have been stuck in here."

"Bitchin' about it isn't gonna change anything," said Jeff Barker, the tall, lean pre-med student, who rarely spoke up.

"I don't need your advice," snapped Lex, glaring.

"Let it go, Lex," said Todd, rising from his bunk and leaning in the corner.

The farm boy from Minnesota continued, "I came here to help people, like you all did. But now we're being held in jail by a ruthless dictator who doesn't give a damn about his people. Why did the Peace Corps even send us to this area in the first place? Didn't they know what was going on?"

"Well, first of all, Lex," explained their leader, "the arrangements were mostly made during the regime of Sefu Abadd, who was a different animal, and seemed genuinely interested in making his country a better place for all. But things changed. Rapidly. And we got caught short. The new Obutu regime, through all the official channels, indicated that they welcomed Corps involvement. But clearly he has his own agenda, and we don't really know what it is."

"This is all a load of crap," Lex declared. "Where is our government? Why didn't they send the Marines?"

Scott looked around the cell at all of them and said, "Guys. We have to keep it together. Stay focused. Show that we're made of sterner stuff."

Lex stood up and waved his hand in vexation. "Y'know what, Scott, I'm tired of your Susie Sunshine crap already. You're only saying that 'cuz you're the area supervisor and you have to say stuff like that. They're not gonna let us out. We're gonna die here."

"You can't take that defeatist attitude," their leader retorted.

"Just admit it. You're scared, too."

"Shut up about it already," Todd said, from the corner.

"No, I just wanna hear him say it," Lex replied. He turned to their supervisor and said, "C'mon, Scott. Admit it. You're scared, too. Aren't ya? Huh? Aren't ya?"

Scott looked down and said, "Yes, I'm scared, too. Who wouldn't be?"

Todd said, "Leave him alone, Lex. Leave us all alone already. Keep it to yourself."

The wiry farm boy turned to step over to where the lanky engineer leaned in the corner. "You wanna make me?"

Todd stood erect and said, "Let it go. Back off, Lex."

Lex sneered, "Oh? Tough guy? Why don't you make me?"

Todd said, "We've all had it, man. Give it a rest."

Lex jabbed his finger into Todd's shoulder and repeated, "Make me."

Todd had had enough. He hauled off and smacked Lex in the face with a right cross, leaving a red mark. Lex went for him, and they grappled. They slammed into an upper cot and then fell to the floor, rolling and scuffling. One of the guards shouted at them through the bars to stop. He shouted in his own tongue, but they all understood, even the cursing.

Scott rushed over and began to pull them apart. After a moment or two of tussling, they parted and turned away from each other.

"Hey! Guys!" Scott said. "This is exactly what they want us to do."

"What is?" Eric asked.

"Fall apart. Turn on each other. It's entertaining to them. And it makes us look weak."

A moody silence descended on the men's cell. The only sound Eric heard was sobbing. He turned to look over the block wall to see Cathie and Judy watching them. He walked over to look at Judy between the bars running from the top of the dividing wall to the ceiling. She was visibly upset.

Eric looked at her pained expression. He wanted to say something comforting, but all he could think of was, "Take it easy."

She looked at him with the pale green eyes that had so often captivated him but were now reddened, tears streaming down her flushed cheeks, and said, "I just want to go home."

Chapter 13

ATTACK

By late afternoon of the fifth day out from Opar, the Waziri expedition had crossed the barren, rocky plain and scaled the first range of hills on their journey home. Because of the added burden of the gold upon their backs, the going was more strenuous than it had been on the way out, and to compensate, the men rested more often.

Their path led them up and across a stretch of craggy hills. They had spent most of the morning scaling the rocky escarpments, and when they reached the top of the highest one, they stopped to rest.

It was an extraordinarily beautiful spot, a wide flat open area on the crest of the huge rocky hill, surrounded by jagged outcroppings and scrub brush. At this elevation, the air was pleasantly cooler, though the sky was sunny and nearly cloudless. No better place to rest, they thought. They unslung their harnesses and lay them on the ground. They sat in knots of four or five, idly chatting, enjoying the soft breeze and the feel of the sun on their sore muscles.

Tarzan stood near the edge of the south slope and admired the rugged beauty before him. From both sides of the crest on which he stood, walls of primitive forest sloped down to valleys and basins that were carpeted with verdant trees stretching on for miles before thinning out near the meandering banks of the river sparkling in the sun far below. Beyond the river, the carpet of forest rose and swelled again, only to thin out near the summit of a mountain range in the distance. It was one of the most stunning vistas he had ever beheld.

Dajan joined him and also gazed down at the view for a moment. "Makes you not want to leave, doesn't it?" he said.

"Yes," replied Tarzan. "If only we were not on a mission."

Dajan asked, "Do you think we will make it back in time, Tarzan?"

"At this rate, we should," the ape man smiled. Then, suddenly, he cocked his head to look up. At nearly the same instant, a tribesman broke off his joking banter in mid-sentence to look up and to the west, and then another turned to look, wide-eyed.

Off in the distance they heard a great humming like the buzz of some giant wasp. The rest of them looked to the west to see, silhouetted against the afternoon sun, three black specks in the sky, growing larger by the moment. Next they heard the distinctive *thwump thwump thwump* and recognized what was approaching—helicopters!

Three UH-1 "Huey" military helicopters from Obutu's tiny air force were bearing down on them.

"Take cover!" Dajan shouted. They hastily grabbed their weapons and scattered for the cover of the nearest boulders and brush.

The first copter swooped in like a great bird of prey, except that instead of claws on its talons, it bore high-powered machine guns spraying a hail of bullets that peppered the ground in two deadly parallel trails. Barely a minute passed between the time Tarzan and the Waziri ran or dived for cover and the moment the helicopter soared over them, huge and low and menacing, spraying death.

Three warriors were hit. There was little time to attend to them, because as the first copter soared off over the valley and maneuvered to swing around, the second bore in on the party on the mountaintop. Tarzan and the warriors had only enough time to secure their positions behind the largest rocks and most advantageous cover they could find in the minute or two before the second copter struck. This one did not have mounted machine guns, but it carried at least a half-dozen soldiers who stood or sat in the cargo area in the center of the fuselage and fired down at the party from the open side panel doors. Their fire was more erratic than the strafing from the first copter, but they sprayed death nonetheless. Two Waziri warriors were cut down before it, too, passed overhead and veered off to reposition itself.

The party had been compelled to abandon their precious cargo of gold bars and harnesses in a fairly open section on the mountain's crest where minutes ago they had been enjoying the scenery. Now they were trapped in four clusters, each several yards from their gold. They had their weapons, but of what use were they against the high-powered armaments of the Hueys?

Tarzan knew enough about military aircraft to wonder how these copters, with little more than two hundred gallons of fuel apiece, could possibly expect to fly the distance from Lumbazo to anywhere near the desolate regions of Opar and return. When he saw the third copter come into view, his question was answered. This one was essentially a flying gasoline can, with a huge fuel tank affixed to either side, evidently enough to refuel itself and the others en route. It arrived third because it flew straighter and more slowly than the others. The pilot was presumably trying to conserve his own fuel supply, given the extra weight.

But it, too, carried armed soldiers. It made a pass over the crest, and several soldiers on board cut loose with submachine guns, though only ineffectually spraying dirt and rocks near the Waziri places of concealment, before it roared out of range.

Tarzan," said one of the tribesmen, "why do they attack us?"

"I can only guess," replied the ape man, "but I would say to wreak vengeance. Obutu must have been angered by our attack on his patrol. You know how volatile he is."

"But how could he know?" said another.

"I do not know," replied the ape man. "He must have found out."

Seeing it recede in the distance before turning to regroup, Tarzan had an idea. He turned to Dajan and said, "Where is the dynamite?"

"Here." Dajan reached for one of the satchels containing explosives. The ape man looked inside and saw about a dozen red-brown sticks. He picked up one and reached for some duct tape from the nearby accessories bag. Drawing one of his arrows from his quiver, he proceeded to tape a stick of dynamite to his arrow. He then fitted the arrow into his great bow and looked up. He saw that the fuel-tank-laden helicopter had come about and was heading back to their position to make another pass at them.

The commander of the squadron was on board this aircraft, a man eager to please his general with a quick and successful raid. His observation on the first run had convinced him that the tribesmen possessed only primitive bows and spears, and thus he had concluded that they were easy prey. Captain Batuuli had been a friend of his, and his loss in the jungle at the hands of these barbarous Waziri made the commander gratified that General Obutu had chosen him for this vengeance mission. He would bring back gold and glory. And fuel tanks or not, he wanted to get his shots in.

Several of the Waziri bowmen got the idea and quickly followed suit, affixing dynamite sticks to their arrows. As Tarzan and the other bowmen one by one drew back their arrows and took aim at the approaching aircraft, a tribesman struck matches and held them to the fuses to ignite them. Each fuse, in turn, hissed to life with sparks and smoke.

The copter flew in low for a quick strafing run. From behind their rocks of concealment, Tarzan and the bowmen held their bowstrings taut and waited for the opportune moment. Not only would they have to be accurate, but timing was critical, since the fuses must not run out too late—or too soon. When the charging aircraft was within range, they released. Some missed, but two or three struck home.

The hilltop shook with the thunderous fireball that exploded, sending out cascades of flame and debris and searing heat in all directions. The fireball dissipated into flaming hunks of rubble and smoking shards of metal that were sent spinning and spiraling downward in contrails of smoke to disappear into the foliage of the valley below.

The other two helicopters veered away for a moment, giving the Waziri an interval of respite. Emboldened by their success with the first copter, they fitted more arrows with dynamite sticks and waited for the next one to charge in. And it did. Its crew undaunted by the explosion of their comrades, or perhaps enraged by it, the first helicopter, the one with mounted machine guns, swung about over the forested valley and advanced in on the Waziri's position.

This aircraft was more heavily armed, and as it charged, it fired bursts from its mounted guns. It was not really aiming at the party of Waziri. It sprayed concentrated bursts around and near the abandoned piles of gold bars. The strategy was evidently to keep the Waziri in the bushes and away from the gold.

The copter made its rapid pass over their position and out over the valley beyond before the Waziri bowmen could fire. No Waziri had been hit, either. They had simply been pinned down, away from the gold. As the copter turned and headed in for another pass, the Waziri steadied themselves, bows drawn, for the next opportunity.

Tarzan sighted his arrow carefully, leading with it to match the speed of the incoming aircraft, aiming for the center of the fuselage. A soldier knelt in the open doorway and pointed his submachine gun at a knot of Waziri about twenty feet away from the ape man. When the helicopter got close enough, only a few yards above ground level, the soldier cut loose with a volley that sprayed bullets along the rock and brush concealing the huddled warriors. Among them, two warriors screamed and fell, bloodied. At that instant, Tarzan let fly. His deadly missile flew straight and true, impaling the torso of the murderous attacker an instant before the stick of dynamite went off.

The entire aircraft exploded, spewing flame and metal fragments and pieces of gore in every direction. Cries and screams from the men aboard mingled briefly with the whine of the stalled engine. The flaming copter hovered for an instant in midair before it plunged down into the valley, where it rolled and tumbled down the rugged slopes, belching thick black smoke.

The shock waves from the mid-air explosion rocked the remaining Huey, which hovered menacingly off to the southeast. The soldiers aboard it had obviously become vengeful and angry. Spewing curses and oaths, they blazed away from the open side doors with their assault rifles as their aircraft barreled in toward the mountaintop. The Waziri remained huddled behind their protective boulders, pinned down, as the hail of bullets spattered the dirt and chipped the rocks.

In a moment, Tarzan and the tribesmen could see the strategy. The crew of the copter was not interested in repeated strafing. They wanted to secure the gold and get away as quickly as possible, to salvage the mission. To that end, the copter moved in as the pilot attempted to land on open space a few yards from where the gold bars were piled.

The unpredictable wind currents and updrafts from the mountainside made it difficult for him to set the huge copter down. It swung back and forth like a hammock a few feet above the ground as it hovered. Nevertheless, four of the six soldiers on board leaped out. Two opened fire, panning their weapons back and forth to lay down a spread of bullets to keep the concealed Waziri at bay. Their bullets whizzed through the air and ricocheted off boulders. The other two began to seize gold bars and pass them to the two waiting on board.

Twenty crouched Waziri bowmen surreptitiously nocked arrows into their bows. They waited, watching carefully up from the concealment of the boulders. They noticed that the two soldiers laid down cover fire only in intermittent bursts, not steady ones, stopping every few moments to reposition themselves or check their comrades' progress.

The Waziri bowmen waited for the moment when both gunmen paused. They did not have long to wait. Seizing upon that instant, the warriors broke cover and loosed their arrows. Four arrows hit one of the shooters, and he went down. His mate turned, shocked. Then he too was stuck like a pincushion before he could level his gun and retaliate. He grimaced in agony and slumped to the ground.

Not waiting for the Waziri to reload, the two soldiers loading the gold dropped their load and ran for the hovering helicopter. Curses and shouts for the pilot to take off got halfway out of their mouths before they too were cut down by Waziri arrows.

In an instant, Tarzan calculated the situation. He realized that if the copter got away, the vengeful pilot could swing around again and the remaining riflemen would strafe them. They had no more sticks of dynamite, and it would be only a matter of time before most if not all the expedition would be cut down.

Two soldiers, plus the pilot, remained on board.

Arrows and spears could not get to them if they took off.

The copter was still hovering a few feet above the ground, but only because one of the men aboard was unclenching the now-dead hands of his comrade from the base of the doorway.

Tarzan had an instant to move. He ran, dashing across the open space to the copter. Just as it was lifting off, he leaped and grabbed for the edge of the fuselage floor.

The copter rose up, the ape man clinging from the side.

One of the two soldiers left in the aircraft crouched down to try to loosen Tarzan's grip and push him off. But with a mighty lunge, the ape man snaked his powerful right arm up, seized the calf of the crouching soldier, and with a forceful pull yanked him out of the open doorway. The soldier fell screaming and thrashing down to the forest below, along with the eight or nine bars of gold the crew had managed to load.

With all the apelike agility that he could still summon, Tarzan next swung himself up and into the doorway of the aircraft. Seeing him aboard, the other soldier in the bay lunged toward him. Tarzan deftly grasped the man by the throat, shook him violently and cast him down to the steel floor. The soldier moved to rise and attack again, but by then Tarzan had swiftly drawn his knife and plunged it into his enemy's torso. He then shoved that soldier, too, out of the doorway and sent him plummeting down to valley below.

"Stop!" he heard from the cockpit. He looked up to see the pilot holding a .45 pistol at arm's length while awkwardly holding the cyclic stick with his knee to keep the craft moving forward. "Get back."

The ape man hit the deck and rolled toward the side of the bay, with open door panels on either side of him. The pilot, a few feet in front of him, wavered in his aim for a moment in the aircraft that was now hundreds of feet in the air and gaining speed as it rushed forward.

"Watch where you are going!" the ape man shouted.

The Huey began to rock unsteadily, and the pilot realized that he could not keep his eye on the intruder behind him and the course ahead of him at the same time. He was compelled to turn and look forward out of the cockpit to make maneuvering corrections with the hand he had on the controls. He did so quickly, and looked back to say to Tarzan, "Stay where you are!"

Tarzan stared for an instant into the eyes of the pilot, waiting. The pilot stared at him from behind the pistol in his outstretched arm. He hesitated to fire only because he knew it could be dangerous to discharge his pistol in the cabin and miss.

The floor beneath the ape man began to list. The pilot turned his attention back to the instruments. Tarzan started forward, but the pilot wheeled around and fired, though the bullet hit only the fuselage plating. Tarzan froze for the moment.

"Land, or we will both die!" the ape man shouted.

A moment later the pilot had to turn again to mind the controls, and Tarzan made his lunge. He grasped the pilot's head in both of his powerful hands, and wrenched the head until the neck snapped. The pilot slumped down into his chair.

The ape man now had a new problem. He knew that the unguided helicopter would plummet in and crash in a matter of moments, and though he had airplane pilot experience, he could not fly a helicopter. He would have to bail out.

He picked up his dropped knife and sheathed it. Gripping an overhead conduit for stability, he stood in the open side panel of the fuselage, watching, tensed and focused. The copter was flying erratically, still hundreds of feet above the surface of the trees, but angling rapidly downward toward the vast forest of green that loomed ever closer with each second.

The copter began to pitch and yaw over the jungle landscape below him. Tarzan watched the leafy treetops approach as the descending copter picked up speed, the engine whining, the treetops surging closer, closer, until the copter pitched erratically, careening, and he could wait no longer.

Poised in the open doorway, Tarzan saw that in a second the copter would pass over a particularly tall, leafy jungle giant.

He waited for the moment. And then he jumped.

"He waited for the moment. And then he jumped."

Chapter 14

PROTEST

The late afternoon streets of Lumbazo were busy. Shops were closing for the day, and street traffic swelled as citizens poured out of buildings and took to the streets, mingling with bicycles, pushcarts, and a smattering of automobiles. Among all the usual bustle and traffic, a crowd had gathered near a corner on Western Street to listen to a young man in his twenties named Mtume who was speaking from atop an overturned wooden vegetable carton on the sidewalk.

The speaker was not a new sight to the street corner. He had been there before, several times in the last few weeks. Each time he had attracted more listeners than the time before. The bespectacled, clean-shaven African was dressed in a short-sleeved white shirt and tie, dress pants, and shined shoes, his clothes neat and clean, though clearly not new. He spoke passionately, punctuating his words by shaking his fist and pointing toward Obutu's palace or directly at the gathering crowd.

As he went on, some of the people in the crowd just stared, or glanced surreptitiously around to see how their fellow listeners were reacting. Others who had been listening to him for a while began to mutter assents and affirmations.

"Sefu Abadd was a great leader," he cried. "He promised us a better life. He promised us freedom!"

People assented. A few cheered.

"And where is Abadd?" the speaker continued. "Who has seen him in six months?" He scanned the crowd, pausing for effect. "You know where he is. Obutu has killed him! And what do we have now? Do we have freedom? Are our lives better?"

"No!" some in the crowd shouted.

"No, indeed. Each day things get worse!" Mtume's voice rose in emotion. He gesticulated more fervidly. "Obutu takes our crops and livestock to feed his fat belly! Our daughters are made to whore for his officers! They take our boys to make them killers! How many of you have lost sons to his army? Freedom fighters, he calls them. Do you believe that!?"

His audience, now swollen to more than thirty people, began to grow vocal in its approbation. Some looked at each other, nodding.

"And why does he need more soldiers? Who will they fight? You know the answer. Us! The people!"

The crowd's responses became more ardent and impassioned.

"He needs soldiers to frighten and intimidate the villages, to collect the tribute," Mtume went on. "And to kill people who do not bend to his will!"

Angry cries rose from the crowd, whose numbers were growing.

"How much longer?" Mtume said, and then repeated, louder, almost in a chant, "How much longer?" The crowd began to echo the chant in response.

When he heard a level of response from the crowd that suited him, he changed the chant to "How much more?"

"No more!" some in the crowd responded. "No more!" Mtume called, again and again, until the crowd began to chant it. Their voices grew louder, more resolute. Some raised their fists and chugged the air in rhythm with the chant.

Across the street, from the concealment of a doorway hidden by a large awning's shadow, two soldiers stood observing what Mtume said, and more particularly, how the crowd responded. One, a lieutenant, turned to the other and said, "It was one thing when he was blabbering on a street corner to only a few. But now he is gathering crowds. He is becoming dangerous."

"Some of what he speaks is the truth," his sergeant responded.

"What?" said the lieutenant.

"I believed in Sefu Abadd," the sergeant said. "Didn't you? He cared about making our lives better. But the General has undone much of what Abadd tried to do. He does demand crops and animals as tribute. And there have been killings. We have seen it."

"Be careful, or you will be on report," the lieutenant replied coldly, and spoke into his walkie-talkie.

Meanwhile, the assemblage listening to Mtume continued to grow. Someone in the crowd entreated, "What do we do?" Several others voiced their agreement.

Mtume paused for a moment to let the chanting die and waited for silence. He looked over his listeners and responded, first in measured tones, then with swelling emotion, "We will take our lessons from the Indian leader Gandhi and the American Martin Luther King. We will march tomorrow evening. We will gather at the Water Street church and march to the palace. We will carry signs. We will chant and sing songs of peace. There we will ask to talk." He raised his pointed finger firmly. "Only talk. We will be peaceful. No weapons. We only want to be heard."

"What if he will not talk to us?"

"Then we will go home, peacefully, and we will come back and march again. And again. How long do you think he can continue giving his speeches about freedom and the will of the people when day after day the people show those words for the lies that they are?"

Many people in the crowd voiced assents. Some shook their heads and muttered.

A woman shouted, "What if only a few show up? We will make fools of ourselves!"

Mtume's demeanor grew somber. "Listen to me. Every movement that has ever changed the world started with only a few people. In fact, that is the only way it can start. We must be firm and resolute. Our numbers will grow. Our efforts will spread to other towns and villages. Soon we will be too many to ignore. Or stop. And that, my friends, will be a great day. Make a difference! Join us!"

Many in the crowd cheered enthusiastically.

Across the street, the lieutenant continued to speak into his walkie-talkie as the crowd began to disperse.

From the journal of Eric Benton, December 1:

> *Crappy supper.*
> *Something is going on. There is a great buzz and excitement in the air. We can barely see out of our little windows, but it looks like somebody is marching down the street. I hear drumming. Sounds like a lot of people chanting. I'm going to try to get a better look.*
> *Oh my God.*

AT SIX O'CLOCK THE FOLLOWING EVENING, an assemblage of marchers approached the end of Water Street intending to round the corner to proceed down Main Street for two blocks toward the palace of Obutu.

Many carried signs. Several marchers pounded djembe and ewe drums hung from straps around their necks. Their solid, driving rhythm was followed by a chant, a song of freedom, with the refrain "Freedom! Freedom!" building, intensifying. As they strode down Water Street, citizens stepped into the street to join them. Their ranks began to swell.

After the marchers in the lead briskly rounded the corner and looked ahead down Main Street, they abruptly stopped, frozen in their tracks. Some gasped. Others behind them, flowing around the corner, began to halt in their tracks as well, and in doing so, crowded each other and bumped into each other as they all, one by one, came to a stop, staring ahead. The chanting ceased. The waving signs were lowered. Silence fell.

In the middle of the street, one block down, squatted a huge olive-drab military tank, its turret gun pointed toward them. Parked next to the tank was a military transport truck, and from out of the rear of the truck poured twenty uniformed soldiers. They scrambled to take up positions in a line stretching from either side of the tank to the sides of the street. In a moment they were standing silently, legs apart, rifles at the ready.

The marchers stared, some grimly resolute, but many apprehensive, at the sight of armed soldiers stretched across the entire width of the street scarcely a block away. Two or three voices made an effort to resume the chant of "Freedom!" they had been singing. Briefly, they were joined feebly by a few more voices, but the effort faded.

The soldiers, too, stared at the marchers, some grim-faced, others breaking out in a sweat and endeavoring to conceal their own trepidation.

From the side of the street, the captain of the garrison called, "This is an illegal assembly! Go home!"

Mtume held up his hand to signal that no one should make a move. "We are free to walk the streets!" his reply resounded. "We have committed no crime."

The captain commanded the line of soldiers, "Present arms!"

The soldiers smartly whipped their rifles into the diagonal present-arms position.

"Disperse and go home. You will not be warned again!"

The marchers did not move.

"Ready!"

The soldiers in unison cocked their weapons and leveled them to their shoulders.

"Aim!"

Chapter 15

SURVIVAL

As the helicopter spun in and skimmed over the treetops until it disappeared into the foliage beyond, Tarzan of the Apes dropped through the leafy crown of the trees. The intertwined branches of the upper terraces broke his fall, but not nearly as much as he had hoped they would. He tried to clutch a branch to diffuse the energy of his fall, but he missed. It was out of reach. He tumbled down farther until he landed on his side on a heavy branch. It held him for a moment but then cracked under his weight, sending him plunging downward again. Picking up speed, he plummeted farther, caroming off one and then another of the densely intertwining limbs, down through the middle terrace, spinning, tumbling, too fast for him to grasp onto a sturdy limb to right himself. He landed hard with a thud on his back, flattening a cluster of bushes and palm fronds.

For many minutes the ape man lay splayed on the floor of the jungle, stunned and disoriented. He was covered with an array of cuts and bruises, with leaf and branch fragments matted into his sweaty, soiled flesh and hair. He blinked and looked around without moving his head. Beyond the moist, leafy blades in his face, he could see a jagged boulder a few feet away, and it occurred to him that had he landed on that, he would have broken his back. He felt fortunate that he did not break it anyway.

His vision was unblurred. He was conscious and clear-headed. Moving, however, was another matter. When he tried to rise, he felt stabs of pain. He might have broken a rib. His leg hurt when he tried to move it. A huge gash in his side oozed blood and throbbed with pain. He felt pangs in his back where he probably had landed on gnarled limbs. He attempted to reach back around to assess whether it was cut or bloody, but his arm was too sore for the effort.

The ape man's instinct for survival was as focused as ever, and he knew that he had to get moving. But where?

It occurred to him that where the helicopter had gone down might not be far off. He smelled no smoke, suggesting that it had not exploded. If he could locate it, he might find a medical kit on board with which he could treat his wounds.

He pushed down with one arm to lift his torso and then slowly, with stabbing pains, drew up the leg that did not hurt and raised himself upon it to his knee and then, still slowly, to his feet. He stood stiffly, unsteady at first, assessing his condition. He could walk well enough. He had dealt with pain and injury before, and he resolved to handle it in his usual stoic manner and forge ahead.

He set out, hobbling gingerly at first until his footing was steady, toward the direction he believed the helicopter spun down, pilotless. He did not know how long it had remained aloft after he had bailed out, but he reckoned that he might find it less than a mile away.

Tarzan walked at a steady pace, albeit more slowly than he would have preferred, through the unforgiving jungle. At length, his efforts were rewarded when he first smelled fumes and then spotted the cracked upper limbs of the trees that the aircraft had skimmed over. Not much farther along he came upon the wreckage. The helicopter had crashed into a gnarl of trees. It lay on the ground like the twisted hulk of some giant metallic dragonfly, its forward cabin wrapped partially around a huge trunk, its fuselage listing at an angle, its tail and rotors askew and bent.

He maneuvered around the debris of scattered metal fragments and approached it with caution, more out of instinct than the belief that it posed any danger. He peered into the remains of the fuselage through the open side panel. In the cockpit the corpse of the pilot was still buckled into his seat, but now mangled and bloodied. Tarzan poked around the cabin to see what supplies, or possibly food, it carried. He observed that the craft was evidently old and well used, marked by chipped paint and worn and rusted sections of plating and conduits. Since Obutu could hardly afford to purchase one, let alone three, of these aircraft new from Bell, Tarzan wondered by what black market machinations he had managed to obtain them and how many mercenary owners they had passed through.

After a few moments' search, he found the small, metal khaki-colored box with the scuffed but still visible red cross painted on its lid. A medical kit. He opened it up to find what he needed—gauze, bandages, ointment. He twisted open the cap on the bottle of hydrogen peroxide, applied it to a section of gauze, and swabbed the open wound in his side. The brief bubbling signaled that, yes, some infection had begun. He proceeded to dress and bandage the wound and clean the rest of his lesser cuts and abrasions. He even found some liniment with which to soothe his stressed joints and aching muscles.

He felt weak. He sat down and leaned against the side of the fuselage near the open doorway, thinking that this was as safe a place as any to rest. A moment later he had to revise that estimation, because he heard off through the foliage first the growl and then the distinctive bird-like yipping of a hyena. About fifty yards away, across the area that had been matted down by the aircraft's impact, one spotted hyena emerged from the jungle, and then a second, and then two more, sniffing and snarling and staring at the ape man. They smelled death in the pilot's corpse, and the fact that they faced a living human deterred them hardly at all. These wild packs of the jungle were vicious hunters and scavengers with sharp teeth and jaws strong enough to snap bones. Lions were the only natural predator that could best their ferocity.

Tarzan realized that he could not fight them off. He had only his hunting knife, and though in his prime he might have been a match for them, he certainly was not today.

The ape man reverted to his primitive instincts. From his throat he attempted to produce a rumbling growl, the throaty challenge which he had learned from the great apes and with which he had warned off many an enemy in years past. But today his voice just broke in a raspy snarl, to which the four creatures gave little note. They continued to pace back and forth, still growling and yipping, their rounded black snouts still sniffing, their dark eyes keeping a bead upon the fallen Lord of the Jungle.

Tarzan turned to look inside the copter cabin to search for anything with which he might defend himself. He scanned the walls and the cargo area, and then his gaze fell upon the cockpit. He had almost forgotten the pilot's handgun until he noticed it wedged near the floor, its handle protruding from under the twisted frame of the copilot seat.

At that instant, the lead hyena flattened its black, rounded ears and sprang forward on short, muscular hind legs, launching into a run toward the ape man.

Tarzan's quick eye saw the hyena coming, and he turned to scramble into the cockpit to seize the handle of the .45. He winced in pain from his aching side as he grasped the handgun and whirled back to face the doorway, quickly positioning himself to fire.

The beast was little more than a dozen yards from the ape man when the crack of the pistol's report reverberated through the jungle, followed immediately by the howling squeal of the injured creature. Tarzan fired again, and the beast fell to the ground. The second hyena commenced to bark and growl, but before it had a chance to advance, Tarzan shot it as well. The remaining two hyenas snarled and paced frantically, alternately inching closer toward the bodies of their pack mates and backing off. Tarzan knew that it would be but a moment before a third hyena worked up the courage to charge, so that when the closer one began to advance, barking and yipping fiercely, the ape man shot it down. Seeing its three partners cut down, the fourth creature, either out of fear or the prudent choice to live to fight another day, decided to turn tail and run. Tarzan fired once at the form retreating into the cloak of jungle, not sure whether he hit it. When he took aim and squeezed the trigger again, he heard a sound that brought as much anxiety to him as the initial sound of the approaching carnivores—the click of the hammer against an empty chamber. He was out of ammunition!

He looked around the wrecked cabin for a cartridge belt or ammunition box, but found none. Nor could he find another weapon. This was the helicopter without a mounted machine gun. The danger of the hyenas was past for the moment, but now he had only his knife and his wits to protect him. Nightfall was approaching, and he needed to rest before he could venture further. But what could he do if predators visited again? The twisted doors of the wreck were stuck open, and he did not have the strength to wrench them closed.

At least he could satisfy his hunger now. With his hunting knife, Tarzan skinned and cut off a section of meat from the haunch of one of the hyenas and commenced to wolf it down raw, as he had done with so many kills over the years in the jungle. The meat of the hyena was unappetizing, salty and tough, and he would have much preferred the tender flesh of an antelope or eland, but he was hardly in a position to choose.

Having filled his belly, he wiped and sheathed his knife and, one by one, proceeded to drag or carry the bodies of the three animals and set them at intervals around the perimeter of the area. The pains in his leg and ribs were often excruciating, so that he was compelled to halt several times, much to his chagrin. He extricated the pilot's body from the cockpit and positioned it some distance from the wreckage as well. The ape man hoped that any other inquisitive predators or scavengers would find enough to sate their appetites before discovering him.

His strategy proved correct. He passed the night uneventfully and managed a more or less restful sleep, the pain of his injuries notwithstanding.

The morning light forced the ape man to assess his prospects. He did not want to simply remain here until he healed, however long that might be. He reasoned that the Waziri would not find him because if they had tried to follow him, they would have found him by now. They had undoubtedly given him up for dead, which is what he would have done. More importantly, they had a very real deadline to meet.

He needed to get back. Even if he had felt no obligation to the Waziri, he could not simply stay here. He needed to move. But before he could be any good to anybody, including himself, he needed to heal and be rejuvenated, and promptly. He resolved to seek out old Azi.

Chapter 16

AZI

Azi was a healer. At one time, he would have been called a witch doctor when that term did not carry the disapprobation that it now did, suggesting the image of a garishly-dressed wild man feverishly chanting and rattling bones and carrying on. Azi did none of that.

He came from a long line of healers and was a mentor to the healers of many tribes, including the Waziri. Tarzan often thought that had he been born in Boston or London, Azi could have been a great physician, with his encyclopedic memory for conditions and treatments, his considerable insight into psychology, and his gentle manner.

In his younger days, Azi had been healer to a tribe that had been conquered by another. In the resulting power struggle, he had been cast out in favor of the conquering tribe's witch doctor, the brother of their chief. But Azi was not discouraged. With the strength of character and independence of spirit that had always served him well, he set himself up in his own hut in the deep woods, and treated any and all who came to him.

Azi's ministrations were powerful indeed. Many a day had found a line of people patiently waiting outside his hut. Injured hunters, mothers with squalling babes, and the elderly infirm from many tribes came to him. He took no money, but he wanted for little. He was paid in animals, pelts, plants and herbs, seeds, weapons, or fruits and grains.

In recent years, as more hospitals were built and modern medical care became more available in the jungle provinces, Azi became less sought out, so that he lived his declining years in relative isolation. Tarzan had not seen him in years, and indeed was unsure whether the old healer was still around, but the nearest town with a hospital was too far, and in his condition he could not risk Obutu's agents finding him.

Thus the ape man set out to find the hut of the great healer. In his prime, he could have swung through the trees and made the journey in less than a day, but in his present condition, the going was precarious. He could only walk slowly through the forest, and each step pained him. He was obliged to favor his injured leg, and he had to stop to catch his breath often. Moreover, he had only his knife, and he was too weak and infirm to hunt, so that he became weaker from hunger. Not one for self-pity, the ape man met this challenge with the same resolve with which he had met other mental or physical challenges in his life. He pressed on.

At the end of the day, he sought the shelter of a tree to sleep, but hoisting himself up even to the lower limbs sapped a considerable amount of strength.

The second day progressed to the third. He stopped to rest more often than he thought prudent, fearing that he would fall and hit his head on a rock if he did not. Each time he paused to rest, it required a greater effort to rise and continue. He often became disoriented. At times, he believed that he was near Azi's hut. At other times, he did not recognize any of the surrounding topography and was unsure of the way. He was sustained only by a smattering of wild berries he found on the second day and two small streams he happened upon.

On the third day—or perhaps it was the fourth because he had begun to lose track of time—he was so overcome with pain and weakness that he began to stumble. He fell once on his hurt leg, and the stabbing pain was intense. He fell again later and felt a profound dizziness and fatigue. His wounds were bleeding anew. His injuries ached and his head swirled. He tried to push himself up from the matted jungle floor, but his arms gave out like weak stalks under a crushing weight. His vision blurred. The consciousness drained from his mind as if a plug had been pulled.

HE AWOKE TO A STRONG, pungent smell of incense. He blinked and looked around. He was stretched out on zebra and leopard hides in a large hut with an arched ceiling of timbers and thatch. From racks and poles scattered around its perimeter hung an array of animal pelts, bones, and bundles of dried herbs and flowers.

The grayed, wizened face of old Azi bent over him and smiled, showing yellowed teeth.

"Hello, Tarzan of the Apes. How do you feel?"

"I…I am not sure. How did I get here?"

"Do you remember falling in the forest? Do you remember me finding you and leading you here?"

Tarzan tried to clear his foggy mind. "No, I…I do not remember."

"I suspect you do not remember many things which happened. Do you remember calling out to Jane? Or to someone called La?"

The ape man was a bit embarrassed at the thought of such intimate revelations, but he had to say that, no, he did not remember such utterances, either.

The old man went on, "You are feverish. You have a cracked rib and many infected wounds. You have lost blood. You rest. Then when you are up to it, you can tell your old friend how it is that you came to his door, and in such a condition."

Azi shuffled over to the cooking fire to tend to a bubbling pot and then turned to a hand-hewn work table which was spread with vials and chopping boards and baskets of herbs and—Tarzan could not see them but could certainly tell by the smell—animal entrails. Tarzan noticed that his mid-torso had been tightly bandaged, and Azi had evidently applied some thick, foul poultice to his larger wound. He was not sure whether he felt better, because before his mind could focus further, he fell back asleep.

TARZAN OF THE APES was not certain how long he remained in the hut of the old healer. He was sustained by drafts of potions which, though vile-smelling, felt rejuvenating. Azi replaced his dressings and reapplied his poultices daily, so that Tarzan felt his pain diminish and he came to feel renewed strength and vigor.

"What do you wish in payment for this?" Tarzan asked his old friend as soon as he was able to sit up.

The wrinkled old face smiled. "I can accept nothing. I am already in your debt from past favors. In fact, here, let me give you something."

The old man hobbled over to a corner of the hut, rummaged through some haphazardly-piled blankets, and pulled out a long recurve bow, unstrung, which he brought over and presented to his patient. "You arrived without your weapons, except for your knife. You will need this more than I."

Tarzan took the weapon and studied its handiwork. It was long and smooth, carved skillfully from a single trunk of strong-grained hardwood. Azi said, "Long ago, a grateful chieftain gave this to me. It is a fine weapon. I used it to hunt for many years. Alas, I am too weak to draw it any more. Perhaps it can serve you."

Tarzan stood up to string the bow. He placed one end down against the side of his foot and strained to bend the other to meet the loop of the bowstring, but the pain jabbed in his side and he was compelled to let it go.

"You must not strain yourself," said Azi. "Heal first."

Over the next few days, Tarzan became strong enough to sit up and increasingly move about with little effort and minimal pain. Between the periods of rest which Azi demanded, he busied himself fashioning new arrows and helping his old friend with chores. The ape man and the healer had time to talk about many matters, including old times and how the jungle was changing, as well as the mission that brought him here. Tarzan would have enjoyed these talks more if he had not been preoccupied with his quest. It was not long before the ape man was eager to leave, despite the old healer's insistence that he remain longer.

"Patience, my friend," Azi told him. "You will do yourself no good if you venture into the wilderness too soon. Why such haste?"

Tarzan said, "I must go to Kumali. I must learn how the Waziri fared with Obutu."

"And if this General Obutu still makes trouble for them? What will you do?"

"I do not know. I will have to see."

Azi drew a breath, and his gray, wiry bushes of eyebrows furrowed as he said, "What is this need you have to put yourself in danger, to be the savior of everyone?"

Tarzan looked down rather intently at the arrow he was fashioning and said, "Have you now added psychoanalysis to your many skills?"

"I wish my abilities included that of seer," replied the old man, softly. "But I fear that death lurks in the shadows, waiting."

Tarzan smiled wryly. "Death and I are old comrades. He has been with me, lurking and threatening, my whole life. I have escaped him and outwitted him many times. I do not fear him."

"Perhaps not. Yet there is a difference between courage and foolhardiness."

Tarzan looked away. "I must help my friends."

The time soon came when Tarzan could string the bow effortlessly. Picking up an arrow, he stepped outside the hut and stood looking for a suitable target. Raising himself to his full height, he took a deep breath and drew back the arrow the entire length of his arm and held it, his bronzed sinewy muscles tense and bulging, as he aimed it at a downed tree trunk some thirty yards away. He released. The bowstring sang, and with a mighty thwap the missile lodged in the trunk, penetrating the wood a full three inches. He felt not a twinge of pain from his rib nor groan from his muscles. Grim-faced, he exchanged with Azi a glance that spoke volumes.

He was ready.

Chapter 17

RIPPLES

From the journal of Eric Benton, December 2? (I lost track of the date):

The jail cells are beginning to get crowded with protestors, including some in our section in the cell that Dennis was in.

An amazing thing happened in the street. A protestor named Mtume, who has been speaking on the street corners against Obutu's regime, led a protest march on the palace. They were met by a squadron of soldiers who ordered them to stop and turn around, and when they didn't, the soldiers fired. Some marchers were shot.

But what's amazing is that some of the soldiers panicked and a lot of them held back. Some of them just fired into the air, we've been told. It was impossible to tell which ones did that or how many, but very few marchers were wounded, and only two killed. Many got away.

We don't know what Obutu's reaction was. Some say he was outraged and threw a fit. Some say he wasn't even told about the incident, for fear of enraging him. Scott says that what seems clear is that Obutu is losing his grip and people are becoming disenchanted with him. But does that mean that he will change his ways, or just retaliate?

Tarzan of the Apes made his way nimbly through the middle terraces toward Kumali. It had been a long time since he had

118

swung through the trees as effortlessly as he did now. "Progress" had not yet come near this remote section of central Africa, so that the trees were still primeval, some more than a century old, and their huge, strong limbs grew broad and thickly entwined.

He made far swifter progress than any ground traveler could have, virtually flying in great leaps, catching himself adroitly on outcropping limbs and propelling himself forward with one daring fling after another. Though he strained and taxed his muscles, his exertions produced none of the pains that he had felt even a week before. The Lord of the Jungle was thus able to leap and swing through the branches as lithely as the apes whom he had long called family. He felt an exhilaration he had not felt in a long time, liberated, rejuvenated from Azi's ministrations as well as from the physical and mental respite he had enjoyed.

Little could the ape man know that as he proceeded, feeling the rush of elemental emotions that harked back to his youth and enjoying the momentary distraction from the rigors he had been through, events were unfolding, links in a chain, which would portend momentous consequences for himself and for this entire region of Africa.

One of those links was being forged in a dilapidated and long-shuttered storefront on the outskirts of Lumbazo. The location was sometimes used for clandestine meetings where apprehensive citizens discussed in hushed tones their fears about the direction in which their country was headed and what might be done about it.

At about the time Tarzan was making his way back from his recuperation, the young streetcorner orator Mtume stood in front of about twenty men in the dimly-lit, dusty room and tried to manage a discussion that was becoming more anxious and heated.

Most of the men seated in front of him on folding chairs and benches were dressed simply in trousers and shirtsleeves, nearly always worn and frayed. A few wore a suit coat for the

"He made far swifter progress than any ground traveler could..."

occasion. Others wore dashiki-style long shirts. The young activist looked around at their attentive faces and tried to feel gratified that at least this many were brave enough to show up. Yet he could not help but be disappointed that this was all he could muster.

They were a varied lot. Some were old friends he had known since his school days. Some were as old as his father, gray-headed men who refused to be complacent in the face of oppression. Some had families, and a few of those families had urged them not to attend, though the fathers had tried to impress upon their children that their future was at stake, while quietly out of earshot of the children also telling their wives to stay home with the children in case they did not return. Others were young men whose eyes were full of fire and whose rhetoric urged not capitulation, not caution, not patience, but bold and decisive action.

It was these disparate voices that Mtume was endeavoring to reconcile and unite for a common purpose. These men all shared one conviction—that Obutu's reign of terror must be stopped. But apart from that, they agreed on hardly anything. Some of the older ones questioned whether anything could be done. Younger men were impatient with talk, and they urged action. Demonstrations. Disruptions. Even violence. Such steps were necessary for freedom, they argued.

"Yes, we all want freedom," one of the older men said. "But at what cost? Our lives? The lives of our families?"

Mtume said, "All around us, in country after country, Africans are struggling for freedom and against tyranny. Organizations across the continent are springing up, following the lead of the African National Congress in South Africa. African people are speaking up and demanding their rights."

"You talk in glowing terms, Mtume," said an older man named Joseph, from the rear. "But many of these Africans are dying. Nelson Mandela and other ANC freedom fighters sit in prisons. And look at Uganda. Since that dictator Idi Amin

Dada came to power three years ago, there have been reports of tens of thousands killed. Journalists, religious leaders, judges, artists, anyone. Everyone. Freedom does us no good if we are dead."

Mtume smiled a kindly smile, refusing to be ruffled by the disagreement. "If you wish to go home, Joseph, you may. We do not order people to stay against their will. But our struggle will prevail. We have right on our side. And God."

"The question remains," said another, "what do we do next?"

"Obutu's birthday is coming up," one of the young protestors declared. "This could be an opportunity."

"Let's give him a birthday celebration he won't forget!" cried an impetuous younger man.

Mtume calmly said, "No, if we do something on his birthday we will just stir up his anger, and he will be especially vindictive."

"That's the point," asserted another. "His soldiers are not all with him. My son, who is in the army, knows at least a dozen soldiers who say they would rebel against Obutu if given the chance. I am told there are others. If we make bold moves, it will show them that there is real resistance. They will be more moved to rebel and join us. It's the only way!"

Three or four other voices spoke out at the same time, nearly drowning each other out. "One at a time!" Mtume exclaimed.

At that moment, they heard the sound of roaring engines and squealing brakes outside in the street. Two khaki jeeps were pulling up. A young man seated near a dusty, smeared window looked out and cried, "They're here! Soldiers!"

"Get out! Run!" Mtume shouted.

The assemblage bolted from their chairs and crowded toward the exit door leading to the back alley. At the same moment, six soldiers burst in the front entrance shouting, "Stop! You are all under arrest! This meeting is illegal!"

The room erupted in shouting and scrambling. The soldiers tried to round them up and seize as many as they could. They thrust two down onto the floor. One of the soldiers punched a third and, when he fell, beat and kicked him.

Eight of the group made it through the door into the back alley and scattered before the soldiers could reach them. Mtume and an older man ran down the alley before they were compelled to stop because Mtume's comrade needed to catch his breath.

"This is dangerous!" the panting man said. "We could get killed!"

Mtume said, "We are talking sedition and revolution. Did you think it would not be dangerous?"

The other rebel said, "But how did he find out where we were meeting? We were all sworn to secrecy."

"The general is skilled in the technique of planting spies," Mtume said. "It is a risk we always run."

They heard a noise from down the alley. They turned to see the man called Joseph emerge from the store's doorway with a soldier hot on his heels. The soldier seized Joseph and threw him down onto the ground in the alley. He tried to rise, but the soldier hit him with his fists and kicked him. Joseph rolled over in pain and then rose to his feet and began to run.

The soldier drew his sidearm and said, "Stop!"

"No!" cried Mtume.

The soldier fired. But he aimed wide, his bullet splintering the fence bordering the alley near the fleeing man. He fired a second time, and again the bullet whizzed past the fleeing man.

"Come on!" urged Mtume. As Joseph nearly caught up with them, they all turned to run toward the end of the alley. The soldier fired no more. When they emerged onto the street, they disappeared into a gathering crowd. When they were safely away, they entered a crowded bar and moved to the back.

"I think we got away," said the older man.

"We did," said Mtume, catching his breath.

"He started to beat me, but then stopped," said Joseph. "Then he fired at us, but he fired wide. As if he were trying to miss. And he did not pursue me."

"I have the distinct impression that he let us go," said Mtume's other friend. "And they are not chasing us. They just busted us up enough to make it look good. What is this, just a warning?"

Mtume regarded this for a moment and said, "This could be a sign that Obutu's façade is cracking and that his support is not as strong as he might think. We are getting through. Perhaps all it takes is for a few more soldiers to see the light."

DURING THIS SAME PERIOD, misery spread across the country as General Obutu's army conducted periodic raids in village after village. Without warning, sometimes at night and sometimes in midday, khaki military trucks roared into villages, frightening livestock and sending villagers scurrying. Smoke from burning huts darkened the sky and wails of agony drifted through the jungle. In some cases, the maneuvers were done for a particular intent, such as to weed out a presumed nest of traitors. In other cases, wanton destruction was merely a show of might.

Teenaged boys and girls were rounded up and dragged from their families. The girls were selected for their figures and their comeliness. The boys were selected for their strength and vigor, to be placed in training camps and subjected to a program of drills and indoctrination in the General's glorious vision for Africa.

Protesting parents were silenced with rifle stocks—or with bullets.

But even as these troops carried out their orders to stage raids and commit atrocities, whispers circulated among the troops of discontent, of growing repugnance with the steps that seemed to be necessary to realize the general's "vision."

As for General Obutu himself, he made his presence visible far and wide. He made frequent appearances in town squares, always accompanied by a retinue of soldiers, whose job it seemed was to stand among the gathered crowds to ensure their enthusiastic reception to the general's words.

He also visited the troops' training areas from time to time. On one outing, he inspected the newly-expanded training facility and public detention area on the outskirts of Lumbazo's west side.   It was where the children of the Waziri, among others, were kept. He visited the compound where these conscripts, often as young as twelve, were being trained to be soldiers in his army.

He ordered his driver to stop his Jeep at the shooting range, where instructors were supervising target practice. Many of the boys were awkwardly handling rifles for the first time. When the general got out, the instructors snapped to attention. Obutu approached one young man who appeared about thirteen and who, clumsily cradling his rifle, looked nervously from his instructor to the general's party and back.

Obutu looked down at him and said, "Do you know who I am?"

The boy stood erect and replied, "You are His Excellency General Obutu!"

Obutu grinned a broad, toothy grin. "That is correct. And what is your name?"

"Jahi."

"What tribe are you from?"

"I am Urulu!" Jahi said proudly.

"And how are you coming in your rifle training?"

"I can hit the target, sir!"

"Very good. Now tell me something, Jahi. Do you think you could shoot that target if it were a man?"

The youth's brow furrowed a bit. "A man?"

"Yes. Look at the target. What if he were an enemy soldier trying to kill you?"

Jahi leveled his rifle to his shoulder and pulled the trigger. The bullet nicked the upper right portion of the target.

"Excellent!" The general beamed and slapped the youth on the shoulder. "Now tell me something." He looked at the boy. "What if that target was your father?"

"What?" The boy was confused.

Obutu continued, "What if I told you that your father was a traitor to the state?"

Jahi hesitated, looking back and forth from the target to the face of the general.

Obutu's expression became more firm. He crouched down and stared directly into the Jahi's eyes. "What if I told you it was your patriotic duty as a citizen of the republic?"

Jahi looked askance. Intimidated by this man who wielded great power, who commanded such allegiance from the soldiers around him, he became anxious.

"Suppose you have learned that he is a traitor! An enemy! He has turned against the people!" Obutu raised his voice. "He has betrayed me and he has betrayed you!"

Jahi felt a confused mixture of agitation and fear. He began to tremble. His heart palpitated.

"What would you do!?" Obutu pressed his face in closer.

Jahi looked back and forth from the target to the general's looming visage.

"Strike the blow! Stop him while you can!"

Jahi steeled himself, battling the paroxysm of anxiety welling up inside him.

"Now!" Obutu shouted. "Before he can destroy us all!"

Jahi gritted his teeth. He closed his eyes tightly for a moment to squeeze away his welling tears.

"Stop him! Save us all! Shoot!"

Jahi opened his eyes, blinked, and pulled the trigger.

Obutu stood up to his full height and, with the slightest suggestion of a swagger, said to his nearby aides, "Excellent. He will do just fine." He smiled and turned away, saying, "Let's return to the palace."

As the general and his retinue strode away, several of the nearby soldiers who had witnessed the scene stared at the retreating figures. Their expressionless faces gave scant clue about their reactions to what they had just witnessed.

Jahi, choking his sobs and fighting his tears, bent over and threw up into the dirt.

MEANWHILE, IN THE WAZIRI HOUSES of Kumali, men and women waited anxiously for their husbands, sons, and friends to return with the Opar gold. And the mothers and fathers of conscripts wept nightly for their children whom they had not seen in weeks and hugged their infants who had not been taken from them.

AND IN THE COMFORT of his plush office and meeting rooms, General Obutu made quite clear to his underlings his desire that his birthday parade proceed without a hitch.

Chapter 18

LOST

From the journal of Eric Benton, December 8?

> *We are going to be let out! At least for the day. General Obutu is having a birthday celebration, with a big parade and festivities, and we will be released to watch it.*
>
> *The whole town is turning out. Even our sour-faced jailers are in a good mood.*

Lumbazo's Main Street was festooned for blocks with flags and bunting. Hundreds of townspeople lined both sides of the street, cheering and waving. Many were dressed in their finest garments, including flowing kaftans and patterned dresses and dashikis with colorful head scarves.

Eric Benton and the other Peace Corps volunteers were released from their cells at noon and led out into the street in front of the detention building. It was explained to them in halting but nevertheless quite specific English that several rifles were trained on them and that any attempt to make a break was foolhardy. Moreover, they were being allowed to witness the festivities only through the beneficence of His Excellency, and it would be prudent to show their gratitude with some positive expressions of waving and applause when his cortege came by.

The parade was long and festive. The air resounded with the brass and drums of marching bands. Confetti and paper streamers rained over the streets and sidewalks. Colorful floats rolled by one after another, bearing costumed dancers and drummers from traditional tribes in the region. Jugglers ambled along the parade route entertaining the onlookers and tossing candy to children. And, of course, military displays dominated, including smartly marching troops, washed and polished Jeeps and troop trucks, and two rumbling tanks. The general himself arrived near the end of the parade in the open rear section of a troop truck, resplendent in his full-dress uniform with its braided epaulets and rows of polished medals and insignia. He stood amid his beefy lieutenants, smiling broadly and waving grandly to the crowd, who dutifully cheered upon his approach.

Eric and the others stood next to clusters of townspeople who seemed oblivious to the rather scruffy-looking white Americans and the hardly-inconspicuous guards posted nearby. The young Americans relished the open air and the colors and sounds. It was easy to forget for a moment their tedious captivity and get lost in the music and the jubilance. It was the most relaxed they had felt in a long time.

As they chatted amiably while the first of the bands and floats went by, from out in the street they heard, "Smile! Wave!" They looked out a few yards in front of them to see one of Obutu's soldiers smiling broadly and making uplifting gestures to the group. "We make movie! You are on camera!"

Next to him was another soldier with a shoulder-mounted sixteen-millimeter film camera trained upon them. Instinctively, the group smiled and waved like tourists for the photographer. The soldiers shot several minutes' worth of footage of the Peace Corps volunteers and then moved on, cheerfully waving in gratitude.

It was but a moment after they had passed that Scott blurted, "Oh my God, we're idiots!"

"Why?" asked Jeff.

His expression turning incredulous, Scott replied, "They just took film of us smiling and waving at Obutu's birthday celebration."

"Yeah. So?"

"So whaddya think they were doing that for? Home movies? They're gonna release that to the networks and the US government. There we'll be, in the newspapers and on national TV, looking for all the world as if we've joined the revolution and are having a gay ol' time at Obutu's party. Seeing that, who'd believe we'd been kidnapped and held in jail for weeks? Our families will think we're traitors. Maybe our government will, too. And they'll be a whole lot less inclined to hurry and rescue us!"

"Damn," Jeff said. "We shoulda sent 'em some coded message, like sticking our finger out or something. You know, like the *Pueblo* crew."

Their debate on the appropriate response to their film debut might have continued, had it not been for a disturbance down the street that caught their attention. At first, they thought the noise they heard was fireworks, and the cries, jubilation. But it became clear in a moment that something had exploded, and a portion of the crowd had screamed and shouted in consternation. Apparently, protestors had disrupted the parade at some point about three blocks down. Eric could not see much from his position, but he could hear shouts and commotion. Townspeople who had lined the streets a moment ago now fled, some down the street to see, out of curiosity, and some back to their homes, in panic.

The Peace Corps volunteers looked at each other. Some froze, not knowing what to do. Their inclination was to stay where they were, fearing that soldiers watching them from the sidelines would not allow otherwise. But it was not long before they realized that those soldiers, like all the others in the vicinity, had left to dash down the street and respond to the disturbance.

Eric seized Judy's hand and said, "Come on!"

"Where are we going?"

"Out of here!"

It was the rash, instinctive decision of an instant. Eric had not thought it through, but there was no time to hesitate. For the moment, no one was paying attention to what the Peace Corps volunteers were doing. He tugged at Judy's hand. The other volunteers had scattered, and he could not take the time to see where. He and Judy saw that the nearest side street was nearly empty for at least two blocks, and they ran down it.

Within a block, the din of the disturbance diminished, and after another block the street ended and merged into the edge of the wilderness bordering the town. They plowed through the scrub foliage and ragged undergrowth that marked the transition from town outskirts to jungle. They continued to run until they penetrated the deeper forest, dashing through tall grasses and around trees, dodging overhanging limbs, leaping across fallen logs.

After twenty minutes they were compelled to stop, winded and gasping. They looked around. Trees towered over them, the wind stirring through the upper terraces. The noises of the town were barely audible in the distance. No one had followed them.

They looked at each other and smiled. "I don't think they saw us!" Eric exclaimed, nearly laughing, between breaths. "We got away!"

They continued to head away from the town. They pressed on into the wilderness for two hours, endeavoring to put as much distance between them and Lumbazo as they could, pausing to listen from time to time to ascertain that, no, they could neither see nor hear any evidence of pursuers.

They were, evidently, quite alone in the forest.

They stopped to rest when they happened upon a stream coursing through a small glade. They knelt upon the soft, verdant grasses bordering the stream and bent down to slake their thirst, gratified to find the water cool and refreshing.

"Look," Judy said, pointing to an abundance of fish, some good-sized, weaving and coursing around the rocks and pebbles on the bed of the clear water. Eric looked, wiping his mouth, and then sat and began to remove his boots and socks.

"What are you going to do?" Judy asked.

"I'm going to catch one. You are hungry, aren't you?"

"You're going to catch one? With your hands?" she replied, a little surprised.

"Just watch," he smiled confidently.

Eric waded into the cool water and stood, nearly motionless, for a few moments, watching fish dart around his ankles. Targeting one after another, he thrust his hands rapidly into the water three or four times but came up empty. At length, he fixed his sights on one slower-moving fish. He crouched down, intently following its serpentine meanderings. When it paused, near his ankles, he quickly plunged both hands into the water, seized the fish, and hurled it out of the water and onto the bank. But the effort threw Eric off balance, so that he tottered backward, arms flailing, and fell into the pond with a furious splash. Judy burst out in laughter and Eric, too, sitting in the water up to his stomach, laughed aloud with her.

Judy looked down at the fish flopping limply on the bank, and then at Eric, soaking wet, raising himself up out of the water. "I get dinner and a show!" she said. "What more could I want?" They both grinned and chuckled heartily, catching their breath and releasing their pent-up fears and anxieties in the first moment of unadulterated joy they both had felt since their capture many weeks before.

They next turned to the problem of cooking the fish. They had no matches and no knife, but having lived a month with a jungle tribe, they had managed to pick up a few skills of woodlore. It did not take long for them to find a sufficiently jagged stone to serve as a scraper to scale and clean the fish and suitable sticks to start a fire. At length, a tidy blaze was crackling and the fish was roasted.

"Best fish I ever had," Eric said, smiling.

Their hunger and thirst sated for the moment, they trudged on, putting more miles behind them. As twilight approached, they found themselves growing weary.

"We'll need to sleep," Judy said at length. "But where?"

Eric replied, "They told us always to sleep in trees, remember? Harder for predators to get at us."

"What if we fall out?"

"There. Look at that one." Eric stopped and pointed ahead to a jungle giant, very old, with a massive trunk and huge intertwining limbs thicker than elephants' legs. "We can sleep up in that one. It's plenty big enough. We should be safe there."

They hoisted themselves up into the immense tree and found a suitable crook in a huge limb which allowed them to settle in with their backs against the trunk. They sat there for a moment, getting comfortable and waiting for drowsiness to settle in.

"Eric," Judy said, after a bit.

"Yeah?"

"Will they be looking for us?"

"Maybe. I don't know if we're worth it. They might just not care. They haven't seemed to care about us so far. I don't think they know what to do with us."

"What do you think happened to the others? Do you think they're all right?"

"I don't know. I hope so. They might have been recaptured and put back in that damn jail."

"What's going to happen to us? Where are we going to go?"

"I think we're heading in the right direction toward the river. When we find it, we can probably find our way to one of the river towns, where we might be able to get help to call home. Otherwise, we might be able to make it all the way to Nyumba, where the American and British consuls are. They can protect us and arrange passage home. We just have to survive and make it there."

"Survive," Judy pondered. "That's the key part. I know we've made it so far, but we've been lucky. All we've had is our basic training. We're not exactly experienced at foraging through the jungle."

"Let's take it one step at a time," Eric replied, and then added, "I'm just glad to be out of that jail. I'll take my chances out here."

Judy paused for a moment, staring off, and then asked, "Eric, are you scared?"

"A little."

"Me, too. And I'm cold."

"The jungle gets cold at night. Here. Take this." He leaned forward and began to remove his denim jacket.

She responded, "Thanks, but…then you'll be cold. All you have is a T-shirt underneath."

"Well," Eric said, repositioning one side of the jacket around her shoulder and the other side around his, "then maybe we can share." She chuckled a bit at the gesture, then settled into the crook of his shoulder as he put his arm around her. They sat quietly for a moment. He looked at her, and she looked back into his eyes and smiled. He leaned forward and brushed her lips with his. She turned her face upward a bit more, and her lips warmed against his.

From the journal of Eric Benton, December 9, I guess

It's early morning, after our first night in a tree. We weren't too bothered by animal noises at night. My first morning waking up to see the sky overhead in, what, five weeks? Dawn is beautiful.

I haven't had a chance to write much, but a lot of stuff has happened. I guess I should say a great many things have happened. Dennis said that I need to try to phrase things with more sophistication and not sound like a high-schooler.

I miss him. Damn those bastards.

"Whatcha writing?" Judy's drowsy voice interrupted him.

"Oh, g'morning," Eric said, looking up, and then looking down again. "My journal. I've been trying to keep it the whole time I've been here. I'm glad I had it in my coat pocket when I left the jail cell to watch the parade."

"What do you write about?"

"Anything. What happens. My thoughts. It might be interesting to look back on later."

"What are you gonna write about all of this?" she smiled, gesturing with her hand at their perch and primitive environs.

"I don't know," he returned the grin, a bit nervously. "What should I write?"

She smiled a teasing smile. "Well, you could write about your great skills as a fisherman. How you painstakingly and with great patience drew upon all your vast knowledge of jungle lore to conquer the wilderness."

Eric smiled. "Yeah, if I ever wanna go into fiction."

"Or you could be a society columnist. You could write about what a charming dinner companion you had."

"Well, I did have that." A bigger grin.

"And be sure to describe the dress code?" she said, gesturing at their grimy, worn clothing.

"Yeah, I always wanna look my best for a lady." They both chuckled at their silliness.

Then Judy said, "Maybe we should get going? We still don't know whether they're tracking us."

"Yeah," Eric agreed. "Good idea."

They climbed down from their perch and stretched their legs. Since they had had adequate rest, they forged ahead, thinking it more prudent to spend their efforts covering distance than searching for food.

After an hour, Judy said, "Eric, are you sure this is the way?"

He replied, "We're still going north, which was the idea. And there's a bit of a path here. It must lead somewhere. It must have been made by people. Or animals."

"Eric, I think we're lost. We must be, because we would have come across someplace by now, wouldn't we?"

"I don't know how long it takes to hike on foot to jungle towns," Eric said. "But there are towns, and I'd think we'd run into one before the river. This country isn't all primitive forest the way it used to be."

This conversation might have continued, and possibly developed into their first quarrel, had Eric not stopped abruptly in his tracks.

"Eric...?" Judy said. "What is it?"

Eric stared ahead toward a thicket of brush and tangled grasses nearly obscuring the path. "I...I don't know," he said softly, "but I don't like it."

A thicket of leaves rustled ahead. They both stared at the spot. They heard a great throaty rumble from behind the foliage, and their skin tingled.

From out of the grasses poked the head of a full-grown—and hungry—leopard.

Chapter 19

FOUND

The leopard fixed its green eyes upon Eric and Judy.

All was silent, as if the wind had stopped rustling in the trees and birds sat still on the branches and insects paused in flight. Like so many others who have found themselves in such a situation, Eric and Judy froze in fear.

The leopard stared at them. It smelled the fear. If its primitive brain thought anything, it thought that this would be an easy meal.

As for the twenty-two-year-old Americans, there was a moment when a dozen thoughts swirled through their heads—disbelief that this could be happening to them…regret at having left the security of the jail…images of being lost forever, their fates never known….

But the moment ended. The leopard tensed and launched itself, leaping forward, and charged toward them. Its tawny, muscled body was larger than they thought a cat could be.

Judy managed a half-stifled scream.

And then in the time that the beast took to traverse half the distance to them, something happened which Eric and Judy would never in their wildest dreams have imagined.

From somewhere overhead, a long arrow came whizzing down and struck the leopard in the back with such a force that it threw the beast momentarily off balance. In the next instant as it began to right itself, another shaft sailed from aloft to strike it again. This time it rolled onto its side, snarling. It righted itself again and commenced to whirl around, gnashing at the two arrows protruding from its side. At the same instant, there dropped from the trees above a tall, bronzed giant bearing a great bow. He immediately drew a third arrow from the quiver on his back and swiftly leveled it and released, striking the leopard a third time.

But the big cat, mature and strong and surging with wrath, was not finished. Its green eyes glaring, it turned and looked for a moment in one direction at the girl and boy, then in the other at the jungle giant, seemingly trying to decide which to attack. Eric and Judy thought they heard a deep, throaty growl—not from the beast but from the throat of the man!

The leopard turned and launched himself at the man.

During the instant the leopard was in flight, the man threw down his bow and drew from his waist a long hunting knife whose keen edged glinted in the sun before he thrust it fiercely upward in one swift move into the jugular of the beast leaping upon him. The great cat shook violently, and the man cast the beast off him and onto the ground where it panted and thrashed briefly, bleeding, and then expired.

Eric and Judy stood, eyes agape, astonished at what they had just beheld. They stared at this strange demi-god who had dropped as if from the sky to save them. They could not discern his age—perhaps forty or a little older, judging from the gray streaks in his straggly hair and the creased, somewhat leathery skin on his face and neck. The many scars on his skin and his near-nakedness suggested some wild man of the forest, yet his gray eyes bespoke an intelligence, and his manner conveyed a civilized, rather sophisticated bearing. He smiled at them as he calmly wiped off his knife and retrieved his arrows.

"You killed him with your hands!" Eric said, breathlessly.

"I killed him with three arrows and a knife," the bronzed stranger replied, and then added, "I should have poisoned the arrows."

"Thank you," Eric managed to get out, and then gulped, "You speak English?"

"...there dropped from the trees above a tall, bronzed giant bearing a great bow."

"I am English."

"Who…who are you?"

"I am Tarzan of the Apes," he answered, replacing the arrows into his quiver and picking up his bow.

"Tarzan? I heard of you. Dennis Fletcher mentioned you. He said he was going to interview you."

"Fletcher?" replied the ape man. "Yes, I remember. That did not quite work out." It seemed ages ago that he and Fletcher had sat on his veranda and he had contemplated telling the reporter the story of his life over iced tea on a sunny afternoon. "How did you meet him?"

Eric recounted the circumstances of his meeting Fletcher in the detention cell, and of Fletcher's murder by Obutu. Tarzan scowled at the account. "That is regrettable. I do not know what Obutu is thinking."

Judy asked, "Where do you come from? How do you happen to be here in Africa?"

"I was born here. Raised in the wild. It's a long story. But what of you? What are you doing out here?"

Eric and Judy summarized their Peace Corps work in Tswana, their capture and detention by Obutu, and their escape from Lumbazo. Tears welled in Judy's eyes as they spoke of their anxiety over the fate of their friends, their stress at being lost, and their fears of never seeing their families again.

"We were in jail for like five weeks and we haven't heard from our families or our government. I can't understand it," Eric said.

"There may be many reasons why he would not make public your arrest," said Tarzan.

"Why would he capture us and not say that he did? Why else would he hold us and not kill us?" Judy wondered.

"He may be biding his time waiting for the right moment. It may be that he has already made demands, and they are pursuing it through diplomatic channels. Or your government may be mounting a rescue operation even as we speak. We cannot know."

Eric thought for a moment and then said, "So what do we do? We can't go back to Lumbazo again, because they'll look for us there, won't they?"

"Possibly."

"Where is the best place to go?"

"Come with me to Kumali. That is the village of my friends the Waziri. You may be safe there. At least until we can find a way to get you to Nyumba or some other place where you can leave for home."

"Is that possible?" Eric said, imagining the idea of getting home.

"We can try. I have some influence."

"How far is it? We thought we were going in that direction."

Tarzan said, "You're about a half-day off your course. It's more in that direction." He pointed. "We should be able to reach it by nightfall."

Eric said, "It's early. Shouldn't we start out now?"

"First things first. Can you build a fire?"

"Yes. Why?"

"We're going to barbecue our friend here," Tarzan replied, gesturing to the bloody carcass of the leopard sprawled on the ground. "You find wood and get a fire going. I'll cut him up."

"We're going to eat this?" Judy said, surprised. "Now?"

"Well, we cannot just pop him in the fridge for later, and we do not know when the next meal will come along. In the jungle, you learn to eat when food presents itself. Survival is the first order of business."

Eric and Judy had never before witnessed the entire process of gutting, skinning, and filleting an animal. This tall, bronzed stranger handled the task briskly, wielding his keen blade with well-practiced efficiency. Eric managed to rig a primitive spit and ignite a fire, and it was not long before the loins of the erstwhile predator were roasted over the flames. Their Peace Corps training had not quite prepared them for a meal like this, but it managed to satiate their hunger, and they were not inclined to complain.

Eric and Judy did notice that the stranger pulled from the spit a shank of meat that seemed far from done to them and munched on it when it was quite bloody. The young Americans could not help but be struck by the contrasts in this mysterious stranger who, though his demeanor was civilized and speech impeccably British, identified himself with apes and was evidently entirely comfortable in the savage wilderness as he sat hunched down before them, his streaked hair disheveled, his skin still caked with the dried blood from the beast they ate.

During the meal, the tall stranger became more garrulous. He commended them on volunteering for the Peace Corps. "The Peace Corps has probably done more to help the African people than anything else the white man has sent in," he allowed.

"You talk almost as if you are African and not European," Judy said.

The ape man smiled wistfully. "I do not particularly identify with Europe. I spent most of my life in Africa. I fought many times against invaders or exploiters who threatened the native peoples for their own gain. I have tried to help the Africans live in peace and harmony, yet time and again, violence and oppression have threatened."

Eric commented, "Well, we were told that Africa can be volatile, but we never thought we'd be in the middle of a civil unrest like this."

Tarzan said, "The political climate here is dangerous and unpredictable, and yes, it will continue to be so. But your presence gives the people hope." He gazed down at the fire and added, "Sometimes I think there is very little that a single person can do any more."

Tarzan took another piece of meat and said to Judy between bites, "Do you want the hide? The Waziri can tan it for you.

It would make a nice coat or bag. You'd pay top dollar for it in Paris or London."

"Um, no thanks, I guess not," Judy said, looking at the bloody, spotted carcass discarded on the ground.

They extinguished their fire and got promptly underway. They continued on for miles until they paused to rest in a particularly sunshine-drenched area where tiers of foliage rose upward like balcony levels in an opera house, and long, rope-like vines hung down in loops and whorls like the outlines of so much drapery.

"Oh, look," Judy said as she stopped to admire the area they had just entered. "My God, this is so beautiful," she declared. "It's like a jungle cathedral!" She bent down to pick up an orchid-like flower from among a spray of multi-hued flowers spread over a rather open area they had just entered, where enough sun poked through the tree cover to nourish such blossoms.

They sat to rest on some giant downed trunks.

"Tarzan," Eric asked, "What are you going to do after you take us to Kumali?"

"I will find out from the Waziri what has happened."

"And then what?"

"I do not know. We will see what they tell me."

"Will you go after Obutu?"

The ape man paused a moment to consider the import of the question. "I would rather not have to."

Judy glanced up from smelling her fragrant blossom and, suddenly, she stared wide-eyed at one of the hanging vines and gasped.

Tarzan looked to his left at what she reacted to— one of the curled, draped vines was not a vine at all but a snake loosely coiled around a branch. At least five feet long, its pebbled teal skin glistening in the sun, it stared, hypnotically, at Judy and Eric, gently weaving its head, its thin forked tongue darting out and in.

"T-Tarzan," Eric stammered. "Sna…snake!"

Tarzan tensed at the sight of it, too. He was standing next to the limb around which the snake was curled as it faced the young people.

Judy and Eric did not believe what happened next. In an instant, Tarzan's left arm dashed out and seized the snake behind the head in a vise grip. At the same instant, the hunting knife in his right hand flashed through the air and sliced the snake apart. The snake's body flopped loosely from the limb while Tarzan cast the lifeless head and body segment to the ground.

"Whoa," Eric said in astonishment. "I've never seen anything like that. The guys are not gonna believe me when I tell them that somebody could do that."

All the ape man said was, "The jungle is not a place to let down your guard, even for an instant." He wanted to add, "You were safer in Obutu's cell," but let the thought pass.

THE YOUTHFUL AMERICANS managed to keep up with Tarzan's pace in their hike through the jungle, so that they neared Kumali by early evening. When they emerged from the wilderness near the Waziri neighborhood, Tarzan was aghast to see the charred ruins of several homes being rebuilt. He motioned the two to hold back as he approached the back yards of several houses. He surveyed the area cautiously to ascertain that no soldiers were around and then walked to the house of Dajan and knocked on the back door.

When Dajan's wife Kerah opened the door, her eyes, evidently wearied, widened in more joy than they had for some time as she exclaimed, "Tarzan!"

"Hello, Kerah," he smiled. "I was in the neighborhood and thought I'd drop by."

The neighborhood was quickly alerted to the return of the ape man. Waziri men and women emerged from neighboring houses and crossed their yards to welcome their white ally and his two young companions. Some reacted as if they were seeing a long-lost friend; others reacted as if they were seeing a ghost.

The three were treated to Waziri hospitality, including welcome soap and water.

In short order, Tarzan was bidden to sit with the tribal elders in the meeting hall where the plans to journey to Opar were formulated. They had many questions for each other. The ape man recounted the tale of his survival and recuperation at the hands of Azi and his succor of the two Peace Corps volunteers.

The Waziri in turn were eager to fill their comrade in on all that he had missed. A great deal had happened since the helicopter raid on the mountaintop, and most of it did not bode well for the tribe. For one thing, after losing contact with Tarzan, they feared him dead. They had seen him climb onto the helicopter and had watched it plummet into the valley. They did not believe that anyone, even the Lord of the Jungle, could survive a crash like that, but nevertheless they conducted a search, calling his name and sounding their drum, but to no avail. They believed that he had perished and consoled themselves with the knowledge that the Lord of the Jungle had given his life willingly for them, as many Waziri had given their lives for him over the years.

They had lost men. They had lost some of the gold in the attack. Moreover, the destruction of Obutu's helicopters and their crews along with the slaughter of his army patrol had greatly endangered their families. Some of the wounded tribesmen were able to journey on with them, but others had been injured beyond their ability to continue and nobly chose to remain behind. Dajan reluctantly left them along with a few tribesmen to minister to them, reducing further the amount of gold that could be carried back. They were in no position to linger, because they had to hasten home.

They did manage to arrive in Kumali by Obutu's deadline—barely. When Obutu showed up a day later demanding his payment in full, he predictably asserted that the amount they presented to him was insufficient.

The Waziri learned that a few of Obutu's soldiers had escaped from the camp raid. They had disappeared in the jungle and never returned, undoubtedly the victims of predators, but had first managed to radio an account of the raid back to Obutu. Dajan confronted Obutu. He asserted that the general knew the reason they nearly came back late with wounded and less gold than they otherwise might have. The general indignantly—and quite predictably—denied that his men had anything to do with such a thing.

Obutu then launched into a rage, though whether it was genuine or for show, the Waziri could not tell. It did not matter, for the result was the same. Obutu demanded that they pay for the helicopters. He called the Waziri thieves and liars and refused to release their children, instead threatening to send them to work camps. He ordered his men to set fire to a half-dozen houses. Moreover, he seized every male in the town between fourteen and twenty to serve in his army, and for good measure he took Dajan at gunpoint and shipped him off to the detention facility on the outskirts of Lumbazo. Obutu apparently still believed the old notion that a tribe is demoralized when their chief is killed or captured. That had never been true for the Waziri, but the capture of their children and adolescents was sufficiently overwhelming.

"Did you resist?" asked Tarzan.

"Yes, we fought back," he was told. "But they had machine guns and many men. They began shooting. And we had to deal with the fires. We were devastated."

Tarzan listened with sadness to the tribesmen's account. "It is even worse in other villages," they told him. "Some have been entirely destroyed."

"I can only assume they did not burn my house because they did not know which one it was," Kerah said. "It was horrible. But your return gives us renewed hope."

"The worst part is, no one knows what Obutu will do next," said Mwanga, the reigning tribal elder. "Since the birthday uprising, he has grown more unpredictable, more intractable. People do not trust him, never sure whether he will be in a beneficent mood or angry and vindictive."

"What shall we do, O Tarzan?" asked another tribesman. "We stand ready, but we cannot launch an attack. We do not know how we can fight this and prevail."

Mwanga added, "In the old days, the tribes could unite against a common threat, but now I do not think we could marshal enough strength. The people are too afraid. Obutu is too powerful."

Tarzan pondered for a moment what they had told him, and then said, "I would like to see this. I will try to make my way into Lumbazo and see what I can learn."

"Do you want to lead a rescue operation?" ventured one tribesman.

The ape man shook his head. "I do not intend any operation. I just want to see what is going on."

Tarzan decided that he would rest and go early the next morning. When he rose, he was met by a delegation that insisted that he breakfast on hot, freshly made flat bread with fruit and tea. He was also presented with a quiver filled with well-crafted Waziri arrows and a substantial coil of woven rope.

Eric appeared, putting on his denim jacket over his T-shirt and saying, "I want to help."

Tarzan replied, "You should help here. There is plenty to do."

"But you might need some help. Do you think I can't keep up? Were you going to travel through the trees?"

"Actually, I was going to take one of the Waziri's cars."

"I guess I thought most of the tribes were too poor to afford cars."

"The Waziri have a little more than some."

Eric pressed Tarzan to let him come along. "If I will not take along any Waziri men, who are raised in the warrior tradition, why would I take you?" Tarzan said. "It is not smart to go back there. Stay here."

SOON TARZAN WAS DRIVING a faded, dusty green Ford down a jungle road. He had gone about five miles when, still staring ahead at the road, he broke the silence to say, "I know you're back there. You might as well get up."

There was a pause, and then slowly the figure of Eric Benton rose up from the floor of the back seat, brushing his tousled hair and straightening his jacket.

"I told you to stay back at the village," Tarzan said. "What do you think you are doing?"

"I need to see how my friends are."

"If they live, they are still in the jail. What did you suppose you would do about that?"

"Well, something might happen."

"If it does, I will not be going to your funeral," Tarzan replied grimly.

Tarzan drove the remaining miles from the village of Kumali to the larger city of Lumbazo. He stopped the car along the road leading to the town, but well outside it, and parked on the shoulder of the road. "We will walk from here. It's that way." He pointed.

"Why are you parking here?"

"There is danger of being stopped at roadblocks," Tarzan said, donning his quiver and draping the coil of rope around his shoulder. "This way, we may be able to work our way in undetected. I don't like to walk straight into a place unless I know I am welcome. And this time, I doubt I'll be welcome."

Tarzan promptly ambled off into the brush at the side of the road and proceeded toward the thicker jungle which began not far beyond that. Wending his way through the broad fronds and clustered fern leaves, weaving around the outstretched branches bordering his path, the ape man maintained a grueling pace, and it was all Eric could do to keep up. He almost said, "How old did you say you were?" but thought better of it.

They must have traveled a mile or two, though Eric could not tell. Along the way, Tarzan pointed out various natural features, such as rocks and downed trees, which he expected Eric to remember for the way back. Eventually, they neared the outskirts of the town, as Eric could tell from the sound of voices and activity.

Tarzan came to a stop. "Stay here," he said. He gave the vehicle keys to Eric and added, "If something should happen and I am captured, do not try to save me. Go back to Kumali and get the Waziri. Understood?"

"Okay."

Without further explanation, Tarzan disappeared into the foliage. He advanced carefully, watching for patrolling guards, but encountered none. He arrived at the western edge of the town, the most newly developed, where he had suspected the training camps would be. He was correct. As he stealthily approached, he observed a large open area that must have been recently cleared of jungle trees and scrub brush, leveled, and in some places landscaped. It evidently served in part as the training facility for new conscripts to Obutu's army, since Tarzan observed a field with an obstacle course and shooting range and some newly constructed barracks off in the distance.

The ape man drew closer to the area and reconnoitered. He did not like what he saw.

Chapter 20

REVOLT

From the journal of Eric Benton:

I don't have time to write now. I'm having an adventure.

Dajan, chief of the Waziri, sat in the dirt of a detention compound on the outskirts of Lumbazo, dejected and grim-faced, his arms upon his bent knees. Deprived of his ornamental jewelry or any other trapping denoting his status, he looked like the other detainees, his plain shirt and cutoff pants worn and disheveled. For the second time in his life he found himself locked in a dictator's prison camp —the first being in 1938—but what rankled him was that this time it was not at the hands of a European conqueror, but a brother African.

The detention center was newly constructed, evidently built to handle the increasing population of detainees. Around its perimeter stood a tall and sturdy cyclone fence crowned by lines of razor wire. Inside was precious little other than two shelters and a section of latrines. Perhaps fifty inhabitants, not called out for work detail, sat or lay on the ground. Most of them were younger; he was one of the few with flecks of gray in his hair. He wondered what they wanted of him. If he had been detained to demoralize his tribe, it seemed a foolish and ego-driven move on Obutu's part. But lately the general had been anything but predictable.

The compound was adjacent to a work camp and the training ground for new soldiers. From his vantage point, Dajan could hear and sometimes see the training that Obutu's new conscripts went through, including marches, drills, and marksmanship lessons. The new trainees were nearly all teenage boys taken from the tribes, like his own Waziri boys. Some were housed in the same compound as he, and some in another a few hundred yards away.

Lamenting the fate of his tribe and his country, Dajan wondered what his predecessor, the ebullient M'Bala, would have done. Probably little else, he reasoned. Too much had changed too rapidly. The Waziri had always been a proud tribe with a noble warrior tradition. Many times they had fought bloody battles against other tribes, slavers, European poachers or plunderers, and even Nazis. But they had never been conquered at gunpoint by fellow countrymen.

Things had been different in his youth. Now, Africa was a hotbed of economic ambition and political rivalry. Since Togo in 1963, dozens of attempts had been made to seize power throughout Africa. Civil wars and revolutions had become as common as the changing of the seasons. African governments more than doubled their weapons and equipment purchases from the Western powers. Billions of dollars flowed out of Africa.

As a result, people who once moved freely, hunted and farmed freely, and spoke freely, now lived in fear. Why did people follow Obutu, he wondered. Why did they not see him for what he was? The tyrant was becoming so powerful, Dajan feared, that he could not be overthrown by a single attack. Maybe the only hope was that the hearts of the people would change. But how long would that take? And how many people would suffer and die in the meantime?

And now his once proud and noble tribe had been brought low, subjugated by armed soldiers, their families torn apart, their hearts rent. And as if that were not enough, his friend and mentor Tarzan was dead. Dajan was so disheartened he could not concentrate on thoughts of escape, though he knew that was his duty as a warrior.

It was in this state of mind that Tarzan found Dajan as the ape man crept along the perimeter of the fence. Taking care to stay out of the sight of any patrolling guards, the ape man crouched low in an inconspicuous spot near the bordering jungle vegetation.

"Dajan," Tarzan whispered.

Dajan turned to the sound, and his eyes grew wide. "Tarzan!" he exclaimed, louder than he should have. "You live!"

Dajan cautiously moved to a spot near the fence where he could speak to his longtime friend in seclusion, keeping hunkered down. The ape man bade him to silence with a gesture, and then in a whisper asked him how many Waziri were in the facility. Dajan pointed out the other Waziri scattered among the detainees inside the compound, some thirty or forty, mostly younger teens and children. Obutu had evidently assigned a few women to supervise the children. Some of the children played with them, but many sat alone or in small clusters, dejected, staring blankly. They were obviously undernourished as well.

Tarzan asked Dajan how he fared, but Dajan was more interested in how his tribe fared after the attack. In low tones, Tarzan recounted what he had found in the village, and then briefly how he had recovered from his injuries and worked his way back to their village with Eric and Judy.

Dajan told Tarzan that things were going badly for all the tribes. Obutu had been conscripting more and more tribesmen as soldiers, especially younger boys, whom he felt he could indoctrinate more effectively.

"Dajan, who is it?" asked a voice from farther within the compound.

A strapping man in his twenties, with a rounded face covered by a scruffy black beard and crowned with a mass of unruly, curly black hair, approached, keeping low. "Tarzan, this is

Adongo," Dajan said. "His family is Waziri. He is one of the rebels."

Adongo said, "I have heard of you, O Tarzan. You can help us. We could use you in our rebellion."

"What rebellion? You are locked up."

"I am but one. There are many of us," he said, looking with dark, piercing eyes. "In the past few weeks, rebels have been undermining Obutu more and more. We have caches of weapons. We have explosives. But most important, we have the hearts of the people, something Obutu thinks he has but in truth has lost."

"How can you hope to overthrow Obutu?" Tarzan asked. "He has powerful forces."

"That is just it. His power is weakening. Dajan does not agree with me, but I know there are soldiers within Obutu's own ranks who would rise up against him if given a chance. He rules with fear, not loyalty. And on top of that, Obutu has become more erratic and reckless, especially since the incident on his birthday."

"What happened then?"

"It was not a great protest, just a quick guerilla operation. Explosives were set off on a timer, to disrupt the parade, and no one remained around long enough to be caught. It was just a message that we are out there. But a curious thing happened. Many more people cheered, and cheered more loudly, than we expected. Anyone who was paying attention could see that there is a genuine resentment toward Obutu, and that the right spark can set it off. You can feel it."

Adongo seated himself cross-legged next to Dajan, and inched closer to the ape man's ear, looking around often to ascertain that no guard was nearby. He continued, "Sefu Abadd was a visionary leader. He would have helped us."

"I remember him," said Dajan. "He advocated independence and democracy. He longed for freedom from oppression, from the evils of colonialism and apartheid. He believed in the African people. They listened to him. They rallied around him."

"And at first Obutu was loyal to him," Adongo said, "however, when he got a taste of the privileges and comforts that power brought, his loyalty evaporated. He wanted more. Abadd did not step down. Obutu had him killed. At first, Obutu spoke the good words, and many believed that he could be the leader that could bring the African people out from under the yoke of oppression and into an age of freedom and progress. But in the last few months, he has shown his true colors. He is interested in power for the sake of power, not for the improvement of the people's lives. For a while, he visited villages and talked with the people. He seemed one of us. Now he has become increasingly isolated, rarely visible except for official ceremonies. Or raids. When he does show up, he has mood swings, one minute smiling and beneficent, and the next getting instantly angry at anything, barking orders and expecting unquestioning obedience. No one has confidence in him."

"But what do you want to do?" asked Tarzan. "Kill him?"

"We must protect ourselves!" Adongo said with urgency in his voice and then, catching himself, added in a more subdued tone, "There have been atrocities. Massacres in some of the rural villages. Tribeswomen have been forced to become concubines for the soldiers, under pain of death to their families. There have even been accounts of a mass grave found."

Their conversation was cut short by an approaching sentry. Tarzan gestured Dajan and Adongo to silence and then hastily slipped back into the concealing foliage at the edge of the jungle.

There is an ebb and flow to the tide of events, with currents and eddies and backwashes that can spur minor decisions in daily life or impel historical movements. Sometimes the smallest word or gesture may trigger consequences which reverberate, rippling the waters like a pebble dropped in a still pond. The decision of an instant may set off a cascade of events, like dominoes falling. And so it was with what happened next.

Though Tarzan crept lightly away from the fence and took but a moment to disappear into the wild, it was just enough for one of the soldiers in the yard, a beefy lieutenant, to spot his movement and call out for the naked stranger to stop. When he did not, the lieutenant turned to the nearest soldier and ordered him to fire at the intruder.

Now ordinarily an order given by the baritone voice of this brawny, imposing lieutenant was instantly obeyed—even if it was to shoot an innocent man. Every soldier in Obutu's regular forces knew that the consequences of disobeying an order of his would be swift and severe. But it happened that the order to fire upon Tarzan was issued to a young soldier named Duni, who had just been conscripted and had had barely three months of training. He was fifteen and had only shot at straw targets and had a difficult time with that. He hesitantly aimed his rifle at the retreating white man, but he could not fire.

"Shoot!" the lieutenant ordered.

Duni could not.

The lieutenant angrily yanked the rifle from the boy and quickly raised it to fire three shots into the jungle in the vicinity of where Tarzan had disappeared. But he heard nothing and saw nothing to suggest success. He ordered one of the soldiers into the entangled overgrowth to pursue the white man.

He then turned to Duni, cursing angrily, and knocked him to the dirt. Determined to make an example of him in front of the garrison, he called over another private named Kinfe and ordered him to shoot Duni for disobedience.

Private Kinfe swallowed and raised his rifle to his shoulder to take aim. His finger felt the trigger, but as he tried to sight his rifle he looked past the barrel into the eyes of Duni kneeling in the dirt. Kinfe was only sixteen, and he had never shot another person. Moreover, he and Duni were from the same tribe and had been boyhood friends, seized by Obutu's troops on the same afternoon. The boy on the ground stared at the rifle barrel pointed at him and began to weep, begging for his life. Kinfe began to tremble and perspire, staring only at the young private. He was frozen in horror.

"Shoot him!" the deep voice of the lieutenant bellowed.

An agonizing moment passed for Kinfe as he trembled, but he could not pull the trigger. Not against his innocent friend. Not for Obutu or the cause or anything else.

"Coward!" the lieutenant spat and then seized the rifle and began to level it at the boy.

Kinfe said, "No!" and knocked the rifle barrel upward. It discharged into the sky. Kinfe grabbed the barrel and tried to wrest it from the lieutenant's grip.

And then, like a ripple in the pond that surprised even the prisoners behind the fences, a second soldier only a few yards away ran over and leaped upon the lieutenant's back, trying to bring him down before the brawny officer could regain his weapon.

A scuffle ensued. More soldiers came running. Each soldier who tried to aid the lieutenant was held back or knocked down by two or three others.

Among the veteran soldiers assigned to this compound were many conscripts who had been taken from their villages and pressed into service and who resented their conscription. Many had longstanding grievances about their treatment, all of which surfaced as they became caught up in the heat of the moment and the exhilaration of turning against their oppressors. To their gratification, they quickly learned that many of the regular soldiers had had enough, as well.

The inmates in the detention compound whooped and cheered at what had, in an instant, become a rebellion. They could hardly contain themselves, letting loose a thunderous outpouring of emotion, stomping and waving their arms and shouting at the sight of Obutu's troops rebelling against their superiors.

Some of the younger soldiers, whose sympathy often lay more with the detainees than with their own sense of duty, turned their attention to them. One of them shot off the locks on the compound's gates, and the detainees charged out, shouting in glee at their freedom and rage at their captors. Many joined the scuffles against those soldiers loyal to the general who still tried to resist.

In the meantime, another officer had come running from the nearby barracks when he heard the commotion. Seeing his fellow officer on the ground and the tide of detainees running from the compound gate, he drew his sidearm and fired, bringing one down. This stopped the rout for a moment, during which he shouted, "Get back! Back, or I will shoot you all!" He waved his sidearm menacingly.

The sound of gunfire burst forth in the street, but it was not from the lieutenant's weapon. A dozen yards away, Kinfe had found the courage to shoot to save lives of the children his target threatened.

It became clear that a citizen revolt was spreading beyond the troops' capacity to contain it without wholesale slaughter. Each individual member of Obutu's garrison, veteran and new conscript alike, was compelled to decide in a heartbeat whether to help put down the rebellion or to seize the opportunity to free himself of the tyranny of General Obutu.

A great many of them, more and more by the minute, chose the latter.

MEANWHILE, TARZAN DASHED through the jungle back to where he had left Eric.

"What happened?" Eric asked as the ape man approached.

"Trouble. An uprising. It may be quickly put down or it may develop into a rebellion. I cannot tell. I—"

"Tarzan!" Eric cut him off. "Behind you!"

The soldier who had followed Tarzan out of the compound appeared in the bush less than ten yards behind them, raising his rifle to aim. They both ducked as he fired a shot. In the same instant, so quickly that Eric hardly believed it happened,

Tarzan's drawn hunting knife sailed across the open space and lodged deep in the soldier's abdomen before he could fire again.

"My God! How did you do that?" Eric exclaimed, once again amazed at the bronze giant's speed and prowess.

"The question is why did I not detect him following me," said the ape man grimly, retrieving his knife and wiping the blood off it. He then added in a mutter, "Are my senses diminishing?"

He bent down to retrieve the soldier's rifle and handed it to Eric, saying, "Here. You may need this."

Eric accepted the sleek, black semi-automatic weapon, unsure of what he would be able to do with it. He had never fired one of these before. Never even held one. Tarzan noticed his uncertainty and showed him how the mechanism operated. Eric slung the weapon on his shoulder while Tarzan said, "I think I need to go back into town to free the Waziri children and the others."

"Let me go with you. You may need help."

The ape man shook his head. "It will be dangerous. I cannot watch out for you."

"I don't expect you to. I'll take the risk," Eric declared. "I may be able to get my friends out, if they're still in jail."

"If they are in jail, they are safe for now," Tarzan told him. "If the uprising is put down, you cannot help them. If a rebellion succeeds, then yes, we can get them out later."

"I still want to help," Eric insisted. "I can't just sit here."

"Very well," Tarzan acceded. "Come along. Keep that weapon handy."

BY THE TIME TARZAN AND ERIC returned to the jungle edge nearest the detention compound, the streets of Lumbazo were awash with noise and confusion. An uprising had spread toward the downtown area, many blocks away from the training ground and detention camp. Word of the revolt quickly spread through the town and the surrounding environs, and the momentum built.

It was not long before waves of demonstrators poured out into the streets, shouting and cheering. The ripples cascaded; the dominoes fell. Their clamor, haphazard and discordant at first, melded into chants of "Freedom! Freedom!" as the spirit of a full-blown rebellion took hold.

Unlike the earlier street march organized by Mtume, no tanks rumbled out to quell the protests. Only a few scattered shots were fired. Some of Obutu's lieutenants shouted orders, but increasingly, those orders went unheeded. Obutu's army was in disarray.

In the other detention compounds confusion reigned. Some detainees huddled in fear for their own safety, uncertain at first whether they were about to be liberated or mowed down.

Dajan had been freed and was busily engaged in rounding up the children from the Waziri village and endeavoring to move them out of harm's way. The ape man dashing toward him from the jungle was a welcome sight.

Tarzan joined him and commenced assisting his effort. Tarzan explained to Dajan that Eric could take him to their vehicle to transport any injured or those too weak to walk. The Waziri children, reassured by the guidance of their chief and the white lord, gathered around.

As they prepared to leave the compound, Dajan took Tarzan aside and said, with grim resolve, "Tarzan, there is a window of opportunity here. This is a chance. The troops are breaking ranks. The rebellion is spreading to the town. The troops who remain loyal will be more than occupied. They may even be overcome. If Obutu is true to form, he will hide in his palace. If the rebels storm the palace, they may not succeed in getting to him. But in the confusion, the rear of the palace may be ignored or even unattended. One man, if he is careful, may be able to work himself in...."

Tarzan stared into the eyes of his longtime ally as they both considered for a moment the import of what Dajan was saying. Then he replied only, "Go help your people."

The ape man turned to Eric behind him and said, "Eric, help Dajan lead the children away from town. Take them back to the spot I showed you. They will be safe there for a while. Take as many of the youngest ones as you can in the car back to Kumali. Tell the tribesmen what has happened. Tell them to come. Tell them to send word by the drums, too."

"The drums?" asked Eric.

"They will know what you mean. Tell them to hurry."

"What are you going to do?"

"I am going to do what I can to end this."

Eric looked quizzically at the lined countenance of the man he had met so recently, yet had come to trust so implicitly.

"Go," said the ape man. Then he turned and ambled off.

ERIC BUSIED HIMSELF herding the thirty or forty Waziri and other children out of the compound and toward the edge of town. Some of the younger ones cried. Older ones scooped up the little ones and carried them along while others scooted on tiny legs, gleeful at the chance to run and oblivious to the import of what was going on around them. Dajan, assisting in the roundup, said, "We need to get the children out of here in a hurry. Some of them are too weak to run."

Eric said, "Look. Too bad we can't use that. It would be easier." He pointed to a troop transport truck parked about thirty yards away on the opposite side of the compound.

"Let's try," replied the African.

Leaving the children in the charge of Adongo and the older boys, Eric and Dajan scurried across the compound and concealed themselves in the alleyway between two buildings. They advanced toward the truck cautiously, lest any soldier inside it spot them.

To their chagrin, they discovered two soldiers standing between them and the vehicle, either guarding it or waiting for orders.

"You take the one on the right," Dajan whispered.

Take him? Eric thought.

Dajan rushed up to the soldier on the left and expertly knocked him down with a sharp blow to the back of the head. The soldier on the right was turning to respond.

Eric had no time to think. He rushed forward and swiftly clocked the soldier with the butt of his weapon. The soldier fell to the ground and stayed there. Out cold. *I got him,* Eric thought. *I did it!*

It felt strange, but he could not take time to think about it. Maybe later in his journal, if he ever got out of this.

"Do you know how to drive this thing?" Dajan asked.

"Um, yeah," Eric replied. They grabbed the keys from one of the downed soldiers and climbed aboard. Starting the engine, Eric looked around to see no more soldiers nearby and said, "Uh, we seem to be in the clear here for a moment. I think my friends are still in jail. It's three blocks down. Can we go get them?"

Dajan agreed, but urged him to hurry.

TARZAN LEFT THE STREETS and once again entered the jungle trees that rimmed the town, so that he might move more swiftly. Unnoticed, he traveled in a wide arc from the area west of Lumbazo around to the east. When he arrived at a spot he guessed was in line with the presidential palace, he dropped lightly and cautiously from the trees and made his way into the neighborhoods along the edges of town. He concealed his progress through the streets as best he could by moving in the shadows or along the sides of buildings, his keen senses alert to any noise or movement in his vicinity. Few people could be seen in the area. They all seemed to have left their houses and moved out onto the main streets of downtown.

It was not long before the rear of Obutu's palace loomed in front of him. From the concealment of shrubbery next to a garage about a half block away, Tarzan noted that the area closest to him consisted of a small courtyard and an alley with utility garages and garbage bins. Two uniformed guards patrolled the courtyard, pacing back and forth, cradling rifles.

Tarzan watched the guard's movements. Then with precision timing, he crouched down, ran in low, and concealed himself behind a dumpster only a few yards from the courtyard. He was certain they had not seen or heard him. He waited until they were within view and then drew and nocked an arrow. This had to be silent and quick.

When one of the guards turned so that most of his torso was exposed, the ape man let fly with an arrow that sailed across the space and lodged in his chest. The guard winced and fell. The other guard turned toward the direction of the arrow and leveled his rifle. Three seconds later, before he had a chance to focus and fire, a second arrow sailed across and dropped him. Tarzan then ran to the courtyard and dragged the guards' bodies out of view.

Tarzan next turned to the task of reaching the General. He knew Obutu's office was on the fourth floor, but how to get up there? His preferred method of entrance, to drop down from above, was unavailable to him. Since the four-story building was the tallest in the area, there was no tree or adjoining build-ing from which he could gain access to the palace's roof. He knew that he could hardly stroll in the guarded front entrance. He needed to ensure as much surprise as possible, but there was no way to ascend to the fourth floor from here. He would have to get in and work his way up from the inside, a prospect he did not relish.

He found the rear doors locked. The ape man had not found any keys on the guards, and he was amused to think that Obutu's paranoia was such that he would allow his own guards to enter only through the front.

He looked up to see a second story window open. Near it was the decorative end of a beam on which a flagpole sconce was mounted. Tarzan uncoiled his rope, fashioned a lasso, and threw it up to encircle the outcropping. It was a simple matter for the ape man to scale the side of the building, grasping the rope hand-over-hand. He hoisted himself up onto the second-story ledge and, with the agility that was second nature to him, maneuvered over to the window and crawled in. He found himself in a hallway.

He moved carefully along the hallway to the front of the building. When the hallway turned, he faced the end of a long corridor fronting a row of doorways leading to offices on his right. On the opposite side of the corridor was an ornate railing overlooking the grand, gilded first floor lobby below.

Tarzan crept forward and peered over the balustrade, assessing his situation. The large, broad staircase against the opposite wall curved down into the ornate lobby, emptying onto a foyer before the carved double doors of the main entranceway. Two armed guards stood just inside the doorway, one on either side, but their attention was focused on the events in the street. At this point, there was no traffic in the lobby. Tarzan expected that most of the clerical staff remained at their desks, possibly apprehensive about the events transpiring outside.

Tarzan was about to feel gratified that he had the element of surprise working for him when he heard the shuffling of footsteps behind him. A voice said, "Do not move."

But he did move, with reflexes faster than a jungle cat's.

BELOW ON THE FIRST FLOOR, the two soldiers guarding the front entrance, like all the guards in the building, stood nervously at their posts, uncertain of how their fates would intertwine with the forces playing out in the streets. As they watched the turmoil and confusion, they could imagine many scenarios that might occur over the next few hours or days. But they never imagined what would happen in the next instant. They heard a wail, and turned just in time to see one of their comrades plummeting down from the second-story balustrade and landing with a splat upon the polished floor of the lobby.

Caught by surprise—and uncertain about the wisdom of them both abandoning their key posts—the higher-ranking sergeant ordered the other, a private, up the staircase to pursue the mysterious intruder. The private ambled about halfway up the grand curving stairway when, seemingly in the blink of an eye, an arrow sliced through his shoulder and sent him tumbling backward down the stairs.

Confused and anxious, the sergeant hoisted his rifle and began to run up the stairway in pursuit. To cover himself, he fired a shot in the general direction whence the arrow had come, ineffectually chipping a plastered column on the second floor. He fired another to cover his continued ascent. When he reached the top, he thought he saw a naked white man dashing up the wooden staircase at the end of the corridor, running to the third floor.

He did not know how this intruder had gotten in or whether any troops on the third floor would meet this threat. His heart pounding, he crossed the balcony and proceeded gingerly up the oaken stairway.

He reached the top of the stairs and looked around, seeing only the row of closed office doors. He turned to look behind him, when from out of the shadow near a corner sprang a bronzed giant. Two great hands seized the sergeant's throat, and steely fingers clasped tighter and tighter, squeezing the life out of him. The sergeant barely emitted a moan before crumpling down onto the floor.

The effort winded Tarzan more than he expected. But he could not think about that. He needed to press on. He picked up his bow and turned to ascend the staircase to the fourth floor. Just before the midway landing where the staircase bent back upon itself to continue the ascent, he heard footsteps from the top of the stairs. Someone said, in Swahili, "Who's there?"

Tarzan backed silently down the steps, his unshod feet making no noise, and retreated into the shadowed corner beneath the staircase and waited. A moment. Another moment. At length, he heard the wooden steps creak as someone slowly descended. Tarzan waited until he saw the soldier arrive at the mid-flight landing, and he could see that it was only one man, who turned to head the rest of the way down, looking slowly and cautiously, sidearm drawn. "Who's there?" he said again.

The answer he met was the piston-like thrust of Tarzan's steel blade. The soldier tumbled down the remaining steps and slumped to the floor. Tarzan withdrew his knife as the soldier breathed his last in silent agony.

He paused a moment to look around and listen. In that moment, he wondered whether he would succeed in getting to his quarry. His thoughts drifted to the state that things had come to, of stalking and pursuing Obutu now when he had had opportunities to kill him in the past but had not. He thought of the incongruity of his stalking an enemy in a carpeted and pillared building rather than in the primitive jungle.

He thought of his past friends who had tried to help him or the other Africans, including Paul D'Arnot and Captain Reynolds, and of this new generation of Peace Corps volunteers who also tried to help the disadvantaged of Africa.

He wished he had a troop of Waziri to back him up now but realized that their proper role was with their children. If the tide of events turned against them today, they would have their hands full dealing with Obutu's retaliations.

No, there was a certain inevitability in his facing Obutu.

Returning his focus to the moment, Tarzan ascertained that no one else was in the area and then carefully ascended the staircase to the fourth floor.

ERIC BENTON AND DAJAN arrived at the jail building in the transport truck. For a moment, Eric fantasized about ramming the truck straight into the building and dramatically crashing through the wall, but he realized that he did not want to ruin the vehicle, so he just parked outside.

No guards lingered in the front office or antechamber to the cells. All the regular guards had either been ordered away to quash the revolt or they had abandoned their posts.

Eric burst in through the door to the corridor that led to his friends' cell chamber, the door they had stared at for so many hours a day, the door through which had come food and their only respite from boredom. His Peace Corps friends were all there, still in their cells. Their eyes widened in astonishment when they saw him. He quickly scanned the room but found no keys.

"Eric!?" said Lex. "Where did you come from? We thought you were dead, man!"

Eric smiled and said, "Long story. We're getting out of here! Stand back!"

"You got a gun!?" Todd exclaimed.

Eric raised the barrel of his weapon to a position about a foot from the lock on the first cell door and, wincing, squeezed the trigger. A tongue of flame spat out as the sound of the blast filled the room. The recoil, more than he expected, shocked him and threw him back a step. Metal fragments spun and tinked against the wall and floor, and acrid blue haze coiled upward. Its lock now shattered, the cell door swung creakily open.

"Whoa," allowed Jeff.

Eric moved to the next cell door and the next, blasting their locks as well, freeing everyone in the cell block.

"Where's Judy?" Scott asked.

"She's safe. Let's go!"

The group ran out, bursting into the bright sunshine and hearing the throes of the revolt in progress not far away. Scott spotted the tall Waziri warrior next to the truck and said, "Who is he?"

"He's Waziri. Kumali is his village. We're going there. That's where Judy is. Come on!"

The Americans hurriedly loaded themselves into the back of the truck. Before climbing into the driver's seat, Eric told them, "We've got to make one stop. We have to pick up some children."

Eric and Dajan rendezvoused with Adongo back on the west end of town and picked up the remaining Waziri children. By this time, they had been joined by other Waziri youth who had been drafted as soldiers. They loaded as many of the youngest children as they could into the truck, while others climbed on top or decided to ride the running boards.

The ones who could not fit would follow behind with Adongo and the older boys on foot, armed with whatever weapons they could scrounge. Once Dajan was assured that they could get the group back to Kumali, he parted company with them.

The chief had one more task to attend to.

Chapter 21

TARZAN AND OBUTU

The top of the staircase leading to Obutu's fourth-floor offices opened onto a broad corridor. Brass lighting sconces illuminated the gilded walls, and the floor was carpeted with red velvet runners.

Tarzan could see that two guards remained, stationed outside the carved, arched doorway that led to Obutu's office. They stood rigidly at attention, and whether they had heard the sounds of the ape man working his way up to their position, he could not tell. Perhaps the street commotion filtering through from outside had been enough to muffle the sounds of their comrades falling, or perhaps they were under the strictest orders to remain and guard the general's chamber no matter what.

Tarzan concealed himself behind a wide pillar near the top of the stairs, yards away. He took a moment to consider how he would gain entrance to Obutu's office when a soldier came out of a room down the hall to his right. In an instant, he would spot the ape man crouched at the top of the staircase. Tarzan had no time to think, only to react. He sprang up and unleashed a deadly shaft at the approaching guard, and then drew, nocked, and unleashed another at one of the two guards stationed at the door down the hall, before he could react. As the men hit the floor, Tarzan lithely stepped back behind the concealment of a wide pillar. The surviving door guard leveled his weapon and slowly advanced, looking for something to shoot at. Tarzan, having drawn and nocked another arrow, waited a moment, and then sprang out from behind the pillar so fast that the guard was taken aback. The arrow caught the advancing guard full in the midriff, sending him crumpling to the floor.

Tarzan stepped back behind the pillar and looked around, catching his breath and listening. There did not seem to be any other guards or activity. Drawing another arrow, he strode to the door to Obutu's office, kicked the latch that opened the door, and burst in. He saw Obutu in full uniform standing at the parted double doors that opened out onto his balcony, regarding the chaos in the street below as if he were watching a parade.

The general turned and was confounded momentarily to see the tall, bronzed figure in a loin cloth advancing slowly toward him, brandishing a bow drawn fully back, the arrow tip leveled at his heart. He reached for the phone on his desk.

"Do not touch it!" ordered Tarzan.

Obutu stood up straight. "How did you get in here?"

"Back away from the desk," Tarzan said sternly.

Obutu retreated several paces back from his desk. "How did you get past all my guards?" he asked. Then his brow furrowed in recognition as he added, "Are you…are you that ape man? Tarzan? I thought you were dead."

"Not yet."

"You are breathing heavily. Are you strong enough to shoot that weapon?"

"Strong enough to kill you," Tarzan said, keeping his attention riveted upon every gesture and glance the general made.

"My agents who reported from the trail said they thought a white man accompanied the Waziri. I should have guessed. I suppose I have you to thank for the loss of my helicopters and crews."

"You should not have sent them. You should have trusted the Waziri to bring back what you demanded. You had their children. You did not need to trail them or ambush them."

"I do not need to explain myself to anyone!" Obutu snarled. "They destroyed my helicopters, which were only engaged in reconnaissance. They ambushed and killed a troop of my soldiers on maneuvers, with no provocation By rights I should have killed all the men in the expedition and made their families watch! A mistake I will not make again!"

Obutu's desk stood between him and the ape man about six feet from him and about twenty feet from Tarzan. Obutu briefly glanced from Tarzan to the pistol on his desk and back to the eyes of the ape man. Obutu made a quick mental calculation and then lunged for his pistol. Before he could reach it, Tarzan released his arrow, which skidded across the polished desk top and knocked the pistol off the desk and onto the floor, far from Obutu's reach. The general froze in his tracks. Tarzan quickly nocked another arrow and sighted it at him.

"Do not make a move. I do not want to kill you," the ape man said, his steely gray eyes boring in on the general.

"Oh? And what do you want to do with me?"

Tarzan nodded toward the balcony overlooking the street and said, "I want to turn you over to them."

"Them?" Obutu grinned sardonically. "They love me!"

"They do? Listen." They both could hear the growing din of revolt in the street, punctuated by cries of "Freedom! Freedom!"

"What you hear is a minor insurrection, started by ignorant dissidents, and it will quickly be put down."

"I do not think so. Surrender, Obutu. Your movement is dead. The people do not want your tyranny. Look at them."

Obutu sneered, almost with contempt. "I am not in danger. My forces will protect me."

"Your soldiers are no longer with you. They are joining the rebellion. They, too, have had enough of you."

"A few, perhaps, but they are misguided."

"No, Obutu. They have all had enough of you."

"And what if I refuse to go quietly?"

"I will stop you. This ends now!"

Obutu paused for a moment, continuing to stare at the intruder, and a look of scorn crossed his brow. "Look at you," he said. "You are ridiculous. An old white man in a loincloth. And you think you will stop me?"

"I will throw you to them. They will stop you."

"They will embrace me. I am their salvation, their revolution."

"They do not want your revolution. They want peace and harmony. They do not want to live in fear of their leaders."

Obutu grew more agitated. "I do not see them standing here saying this to me," he said. "I see only a white man. Who appointed you their savior? You do not speak for them. You are not African. What can you offer them? Nostalgia for a primitive lifestyle they can never go back to?"

"What they want is a chance to determine their own destiny, not what you dictate."

"It takes more than a strong man with a knife and a bow to solve the problems of modern Africa. Africa is changing and—"

The carved oak door behind Tarzan swung open, and in rushed a soldier who, upon beholding the sight before him, reached for his sidearm. Tarzan swung around and loosed his arrow, striking the man down. Before Tarzan could draw another arrow, Obutu seized the moment to rush for his pistol on the floor. Tarzan had only an instant to discard his bow and lunge toward Obutu to try to keep it from him.

Tarzan reached Obutu's hand the moment after it had seized the pistol. Tarzan grasped Obutu's wrist with both hands and wrenched it upward. The pistol discharged, shattering a portion of the crystal chandelier above them. Tarzan gave Obutu's wrist a mighty twist, and the general let go of the weapon. But Obutu promptly used his free hand to pound the ape man in the midriff until he was released.

They wrestled, rolling and thrashing on the Moroccan carpet. They slammed against the credenza, sending the elegant glassware atop it tumbling and crashing around them.

"Tarzan gave Obutu's wrist a mighty twist..."

The general was a bear of a man, solidly built, and he repelled Tarzan's blows with the fury of a beast like the ones Tarzan had battled so many times in his life. Obutu managed to land several blows that nearly threw the ape man off, but Tarzan fought with a tenacity that years away from primitive jungle life had not diminished.

At one point, the jungle lord reached for his hunting knife, but Obutu grabbed his wrist with both hands and clung, squeezing tightly. Tarzan strained mightily, and struck the general with his other fist, but Obutu, trembling and gnashing his teeth, resisted, until with a twist he broke Tarzan's hold, and the knife dropped.

With a mighty lurch the general threw the ape man off and quickly rose to his feet. He headed for the wall upon which were mounted two large crossed spears. He pulled one from its mounting bracket and turned to face Tarzan with it. Obutu furiously jabbed the point at his adversary repeatedly, but the ape man feinted and nimbly dodged the spear tip each time. They stared at each other for a moment, like two great cats eyeing each other's every move, both panting.

Tarzan feinted one way, then lunged at the general from the other side. His opponent lamely tried to swing the spear at him like a club, but Tarzan broke the swing with his arm and disarmed the general. They tumbled to the floor, going for each other's throats.

They rolled, wrestling, until they neared the great oak desk and the open doors to the balcony. Tarzan smashed Obutu's head against the side of the desk, causing the general to yield for a moment. Tarzan clamped both hands vise-like on the tyrant's throat in the death grip with which he had slain many men and tightened, slamming Obutu's head onto the floor again and again.

The general, gasping for breath and in great pain, retained enough focus to realize his right hand was free to try one last ploy. With the free hand, he reached down toward his calf. He strained, desperately flailing until, after two or three struggling tries, he found the hilt of the four-inch dagger strapped to his ankle. He yanked it out and thrust it full into the ape man's back.

Wide-eyed, Tarzan gasped in pain and surprise. Obutu pulled the dagger out and thrust it again into Tarzan's back and side, cursing the ape man, vengeful fire in his eyes. Overwhelming pain shot through the lord of the jungle. He released his grip on Obutu, who rolled over and began to get up.

As Obutu tried to move away, Tarzan grabbed for his leg, knocking him down. They both stumbled in the effort to rise. Tarzan grasped Obutu by the shoulder and with a painful wrenching motion managed to spin him halfway around, enough to land one hard blow to his jaw. In tremendous pain, Tarzan marshaled his remaining strength, and with one mighty, Herculean effort, he lifted the dazed adversary into the air and heaved him over the side of the balustrade and watched him plunge four stories to land with a thud on the pavement below.

Seeing the fallen despot, the crowd erupted in roars and applause. They quickly gathered at the scene and looked up to see Tarzan at the balustrade and cheered him for a moment before he retreated into the chamber and sunk to the floor, disappearing from their view.

Dajan burst into the chamber to find Tarzan slumped down on the floor across the huge room, breathing weakly, bleeding profusely, his countenance pallid. The Waziri chieftain dashed to where the ape man lay.

"Tarzan!" Dajan exclaimed. "You have done it! We have done it! The palace is secure!"

Tarzan, panting and slack-jawed, attempted to prop himself up on one elbow, with clearly pained effort.

"The... the people...?" he asked, his gray eyes, once so steely, now hazy and barely focused on Dajan's face.

"The Waziri children have all been freed," Dajan said. "All the people have been freed. Your young American friend was a great help."

"...and the danger...the retaliation....?"

"Obutu's men have joined us or surrendered, The few who remained loyal to him and tried to fight have been taken care of." Dajan's eyes widened and his countenance beamed. "You should see it! The people are rejoicing! They are lifting Obutu's body and are carrying it through the streets. They have been liberated! Here. You must see."

With great effort, Tarzan slowly and hesitantly rose to his feet, grasping the railing with one hand while holding his wounds with the other. Dajan held up his bleeding friend who, though wincing in pain, could look over the railing down into the street. He saw exaltation in the streets, chanting and cheering. Drums had begun to pound, and people danced. Pulsating rhythms coursed through the streets. It was a joyous celebration such as he had not seen in a long while. He managed a smile.

He endeavored to stand taller, albeit slowly and hesitantly, to gain a better view. When some of the townspeople happened to look up and notice him watching from the balcony, they began to acclaim, "Tarzan! Tarzan!" He drank in the adulation for a moment, then winced and sank back to the floor.

Dajan propped up the ape man's head and looked into his gray eyes, whose spark was growing dimmer, and said, "A doctor is on his way."

"He will...have to...hurry," Tarzan nearly whispered, his face contorted in a grimace. His breathing came in heavy, short bursts. He grasped the wound in his side, inhaled sharply, and clenched his teeth in pain.

Tarzan of the Apes, the Lord of the Jungle, collapsed. And around him the sounds of jubilation and freedom echoed down the streets and out into the jungle.

Epilogue

F rom the journal of Eric Benton, December 14, 1974:

On the plane.

Finally heading home. Our tour of duty in Tswana was cut short, for obvious reasons.

I can't believe all that has happened. I guess I'm something of a witness to history. But all I can think about right now is how glad I am to be alive.

Judy went home yesterday on another flight. We never got a chance to talk about what either of us wants to do when we get back. I think I might qualify for a Peace Corps scholarship, so I could go on to graduate school and maybe study journalism. Scott and Jeff have actually talked about signing up for another tour of duty. They feel they are still needed and that there is so much more to be done.

The papers are full of accounts of the rebellion, but most of the accounts are biased. They claim insurgent soldiers overthrew Obutu in a bloody coup. Not a word about Tarzan. He must have been killed. What a loss. I wish I had known him longer. He was a great man.

The latest paper I saw in the airport covered the state funeral of Caesar Washington Obutu. Apparently, it was a grand affair. Many foreign dignitaries were in attendance, as well as representatives of the Western press. Photos showed the funeral procession down the streets lined with throngs of mourners and onlookers. They should have buried that guy in a ditch somewhere. Amazing how these things go.

Tarzan awoke to find himself in a hospital bed. His torso was heavily bandaged. IV tubes snaked from his arms, and monitors beeped nearby. He was groggy and in pain. He looked around at the sparse furnishings and saw Dajan and another Waziri, Mwanga, leaning over him.

"How...how long...?" he ventured to ask.

"You've been sedated and asleep for four days," Dajan said. "You were severely wounded. Your healing will take time. How do you feel?"

"Awful. Dizzy. Sore," Tarzan said. "I need Azi."

"We learned that Azi is dead. His heart gave out," Dajan told him. "You will have to make it on modern medicine."

The cobwebs in Tarzan's head cleared a little, and he began to focus. He hesitantly asked, "And Obutu? The revolt? The people...?"

"Obutu is dead and his regime was overthrown. The revolt was successful. Look at this."

Dajan handed him a newspaper. In large type on the front page, the banner headline read, "Obutu Slain by Rebels."

Mwanga commented, "It should say, 'We are now free from the devil."

"One of the leaders of the rebellion, a young man named Mtume, has been asking to see you when you are up to it," said Dajan. "He wishes to thank you. So do many others."

Tarzan scanned the story to see that it referred to "insurgents" who invaded the palace and killed Obutu. "Nothing in here about me, I see."

"No," Dajan said. "A few of Obutu's loyal lieutenants still remain in positions of power. They are doing everything they can to portray the rebellion as a coup by the military and a few rebels. They would much rather people believe that than admit the possibility of one man with knife and bow penetrating the palace and taking out the general and his guards."

Mwanga added, "The AP wire service has even picked up the story and is reporting it that way. And if anyone saw Waziri hustling your unconscious body out of the rear of the building, they are either not talking or no one is asking them. We even heard talk of some of them shooting the corpses of the guards to conceal the arrow wounds."

"Some of the drums are saying that you are dead, Tarzan," said the chief.

"That's just as well," he replied. "Let them believe that."

Dajan showed him another front page. "And you missed the funeral. It was quite the spectacle."

Tarzan asked, "And the Peace Corps people? Did they get away?"

"Yes. They are safe and on their way home," the chief answered.

"I would like to put a bar of Opar gold in the account of Eric Benton, so that he can use it to study journalism."

"Good idea," Dajan said.

Jane Porter Clayton, Lady Greystoke, appeared in the doorway with the Styrofoam coffee cup she had just gone to fill, and said, "Oh my God, you're finally awake." She strode over to his bed and kissed him on the forehead. "How do you feel?"

He nodded weakly. "You were an inch away from death," she continued. "I've been frantic. The doctors say it will be quite a while before you're fully recovered."

She smiled and leaned in closer, stroking his hair. "Look at you. You can't keep doing this, John."

"Doing what?"

"You know what. You can't keep running off into the jungle on quests at your age. First, I come back to reports that you have jumped to your death from a helicopter. And then you end up like this. I won't be put through that wringer again. Promise me you won't do this any more. You have done enough. More than enough."

He said, "But the people—"

"Look at me, John." she said emphatically. "You can still fight the good fight. Maybe from your position in the House of Lords. But you can't save the world from everything. I need you. Healthy and alive."

She touched his arm. "John?" she repeated, staring into his gray eyes. "Promise me?"

Tarzan turned his head to look out the window at the late afternoon sun setting over the plains and distant forests. The ghost of a smile played on his lips.

From the journal of Eric Benton, Addendum, Sept. 26, 1982:

This is the first entry I have made in this journal in years. After I returned from Africa, I put it in a box somewhere and went on to graduate school to pursue journalism, and then life moved on—marriage (to Judy), children, a busy career first working for newspapers and eventually a prestigious news magazine.

I knew I had this journal, but I hadn't really any use for it, so I never got around to digging it out and rereading it. Until now. I have been thinking about Tarzan lately. I only knew the man for a few days, but he was the most remarkable person I ever met. I'll never forget him.

After the Lumbazo uprising and the death of Obutu, Tarzan of the Apes was not heard from again. He and his wife seem to have disappeared from the sight of man. I learned that he abandoned his Peerage, as well as his African estate, without explanation. After the requisite waiting period, he was declared legally dead and his seat in the House of Lords is now filled by a nephew or somebody.

There are those who say that he was probably killed in the deep jungle somewhere by some predator or accident and never found. That's the simplest explanation. But somehow unsatisfactory.

Others believe that he died fighting Obutu and that his death, as well as his involvement with the dictator, was hushed up.

Some suspect that he grew weary of being who he was, not only in London but in Africa as well, and changed his appearance and adopted another identity. A few older Waziri will whisper that he was administered some kind of immortality potion long ago that will allow him to live on indefinitely. Well, I wouldn't know about any of that.

Personally, I prefer to believe that he chucked it all and went back to dig up some Opar gold and used that to live out the rest of his days somewhere quietly in comfort and seclusion. He has certainly earned that.

But his memory lives on, and people will still tell his stories.

I should make an effort to find him. I imagine his exploits would make a fascinating article, or possibly a book. From time to time, in my weaker moments, I think about trying to research them and write them up. I'd really like to know what happened to him.

But I suppose we'll never know.

The Wild Adventures of

Edgar Rice Burroughs® Series

1. Tarzan: Return to Pal-ul-don (2015)

2. Tarzan on the Precipice (2016)

3. Tarzan Trilogy (2016)

4. Tarzan: The Greystoke Legacy Under Siege (2017)

5. A Soldier of Poloda
   Further Adventures Beyond the Farthest Star (2017)

6. Swords Against the Moon Men (2017)

7. Untamed Pellucidar (2018)

8. Tarzan and the Revolution (2018)

TARZAN® and the Revolution

Thomas Zachek grew up on Tarzan movies and, to a lesser extent, the comics. He became hooked on the real Tarzan in high school after picking up a new Ace paperback edition of *Tarzan and the Lost Empire* for fifty cents–the one with the Frank Frazetta cover with Tarzan hanging from a limb on a cliff overlooking the Roman city. Thomas went on to collect the entire series of Ace and Ballantine paperback reissues of Burroughs' Tarzan tales (he still has them).

Thomas discovered that Burroughs' stories were quite unlike the family-friendly Tarzan of the movies, with Johnny Weismuller as the hulking hero living for some reason in the jungle with a classy, aristocratic Jane. No, Burroughs' hero was actually a British lord who spoke educated English and had a fascinating backstory. Thomas was impressed with the superior level of development and action in these tales.

Nearly forty years passed, wherein most of the writing Thomas did was lesson plans, plus the occasional letter to the editor and a series of columns for the *Milwaukee Journal Sentinel*. He attempted writing his first Tarzan tale in 2005 as something of a lark, and then followed it, to date, with six more Tarzan tales. Friends encouraged Thomas to try to get the stories published. Thomas tells us he is grateful to Jim Sullos of ERB, Inc., for giving him the chance. The first three were published in 2016 in a volume entitled *Tarzan Trilogy*. Thomas notes, "This is my fourth tale. I have tried to craft realistic, page-turning adventure tales featuring classic Tarzan elements while at the same time taking the character in directions that have not been done in Tarzan stories before."

We invite you to share your thoughts and comments with Thomas at zachekbooks@gmail.com.

ARTIST

Mike Grell is a legendary, award-winning artist who has worked on many titles including *Legion of Super-heroes*, *Green Arrow* and *Green Lantern*. Plus, he has created numerous titles of his own, including *Starslayer*, *Shaman's Tears*, *Bar Sinister*, *Maggie The Cat*, *Warlord* and *Jon Sable, Freelance*. Mike wrote and drew the Tarzan comic strip from July 1981 to February 1983.

About Edgar Rice Burroughs, Inc.

 Founded in 1923 by Edgar Rice Burroughs, as one of the first authors to incorporate himself, Edgar Rice Burroughs, Inc. holds numerous trademarks and the rights to all literary works of the author still protected by copyright, including stories of Tarzan of the Apes and John Carter of Mars. The company has overseen every adaptation of his literary works in film, television, radio, publishing, theatrical stage productions, licensing and merchandising. The company is still a very active enterprise and manages and licenses the vast archive of Mr. Burroughs' literary works, fictional characters and corresponding artworks that have grown for over a century. The company continues to be owned by the Burroughs family and remains headquartered in Tarzana, California, the town named after the Tarzana Ranch Mr. Burroughs purchased there in 1919 which led to the town's future development.

www.edgarriceburroughs.com
www.tarzan.com

PELLUCIDAR

BOOK SERIES #7

Untamed Pellucidar

By Lee Strong

The Soviet government's Red Army, led by Comrade Trotsky, pursues the retreating White Russian forces into the dangerous world of Pellucidar. Young conscript Kirov, formerly a student anthropologist, finds his escape from the war short lived as he meets the incredible and dangerous Paleolithic animal life of the Northern environs of Pellucidar's Stone Age world. To survive, Kirov must escape slavery from the beautiful Ala and her mighty Black Birdriders, foster a civil war, impress the natives with his "inventions," conquer the terrifying Pulka Horde, and become the warlord of several tribes as they flee the Soviet invaders. Untamed Pellucidar is a tale in the grand tradition of Edgar Rice Burroughs' epic adventures At The Earth's Core.

Moon Men

BOOK SERIES #6

Swords Against the Moon Men

By Christopher Paul Carey

In this sequel to Edgar Rice Burroughs'
Moon Maid trilogy, Earth has been
conquered and humanity brutally
enslaved under the cruel tyranny of
the Kalkar invaders whose evil was
spawned from Va-nah, the Moon's
hollow interior. A desperate plea
from Barsoom swiftly hurls Julian 7th
upon a lonely quest into the heart
of Va-nah where he teams up with a
U-ga princess and a fierce alien quadruped,
and launches a daring rescue to save a lost
Barsoomian ambassadorial mission.

Available at www.ERBurroughs.com/Store

The Wild Adventures of Edgar Rice Burroughs* Series 6

Swords
Against the
Moon Men

Christopher Paul Carey

WV

Sci-Fi

BOOK SERIES #5

A Soldier of Poloda

By Lee Strong

FURTHER ADVENTURES
BEYOND THE FARTHEST STAR

Worlds at War! American intelligence officer Thomas Randolph is teleported from the World War II battlefields of Normandy into the belly of the evil Kapar empire on the planet Poloda. The Kapar's only passion is to conquer and destroy the outnumbered Unis forces who had been engaged in a century-long struggle to survive. Rechristened Tomas Ran, the Earthman now understands that the same fierce determination to defeat Hitler must now be used as a weapon to defeat the fascist Kapars—a merciless foe bent on global domination.

Available at www.ERBurroughs.com/Store

WV

TARZAN
BOOK SERIES #4

TARZAN
The Greystoke
Legacy
Under Siege

**By Ralph N. Laughlin
& Ann E. Johnson**

Set in the 1980s, The Greystoke
Legacy Under Siege lifts the TARZAN
series to new, ground-breaking
heights with a high adventure that
immerses TARZAN and his offspring
in an epic battle for their family's
survival. The book also includes a solution to
the real-life murder of Dian Fossey, who devoted
her life to the study and preservation of African
gorillas. With new interior illustrations.

Available at www.ERBurroughs.com/Store

WV

TARZAN®

The Wild Adventures of
EDGAR RICE BURROUGHS

BOOK SERIES #3

TARZAN TRILOGY

By Thomas Zachek

Three ALL NEW tales, in one book,
featuring Tarzan at Point Station,
a remote English outpost near the
Waziri homelands. Set during the
advent of World War II, we see
more and more European
intrusion into the Bolongo River
Basin. Tarzan becomes embroiled
in increasingly dangerous events
as cultures clash. With new
interior illustrations.

Available at www.ERBurroughs.com/Store

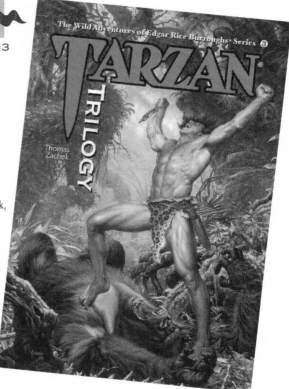

TARZAN

The Wild Adventures of Edgar Rice Burroughs

BOOK SERIES #2

TARZAN on the Precipice

By Michael A. Sanford

At the conclusion of the classic TARZAN OF THE APES by Edgar Rice Burroughs, Tarzan is despondent but assured he did what was honorable by enabling Jane to leave with his cousin, William Clayton (who believes he is the rightful heir to the Greystoke estate and can appropriately provide for Jane when they marry). But what then? There has never been an explanation of Tarzan's activities after his presence in Wisconsin and his voyage back to Africa—until now.

Available at www.ERBurroughs.com/Store

KING KONG VS. TARZAN

JOIN THE PREMIER EDGAR RICE BURROUGHS FAN ORGANIZATION

Edgar Rice Burroughs in 1916

In 1947, Edgar Rice Burroughs personally approved the creation of a fan club and fanzine. The fanzine was first published that year as *The Burroughs Bulletin*, and is the longest-running ERB fanzine still being published. The fan club was founded in 1960 as The Burroughs Bibliophiles, which adopted the *Bulletin* as its journal. The Bibliophiles also issues a monthly newsletter, *The Gridley Wave*, and other special publications.

Today, The Burroughs Bibliophiles remains the largest ERB fan organization in the world, with members from around the globe and with local chapters across the United States and in England. Besides publishing its journal and newsletter, the Bibliophiles sponsors the annual convention called the "Dum-Dum," named for ceremonial gatherings of the Great Apes in the Tarzan novels. Members continue to be influential in all aspects of Burroughs, from publishing critical analyses to writing new authorized fiction, including novels in *The Wild Adventures of Edgar Rice Burroughs Series*.

For more information about the society and membership, visit the Bibliophiles' website at www.BurroughsBibliophiles.com or The Burroughs Bibliophiles Facebook page. You can also e-mail the Editor at BurroughsBibliophiles@gmail.com, call (573) 647-0225, or mail 318 Patriot Way, Yorktown, Virginia 23693-4639, USA.